THE
BEST
AMERICAN
EROTICA
1993

THE
BEST
AMERICAN
EROTICA
1993

EDITED BY SUSIE BRIGHT

Charles Scribner's Sons
New York

Maxwell Macmillan Canada
Toronto
Maxwell Macmillan International
New York   Oxford   Singapore   Sydney

Copyright © 1993 by Macmillan Publishing Company, a division of Macmillan, Inc.

Charles Scribner's Sons
Macmillan Publishing Company
866 Third Avenue
New York, NY 10022

Maxwell Macmillan Canada, Inc.
1200 Eglinton Avenue East
Suite 200
Don Mills, Ontario M3C 3N1

Macmillan Publishing Company is part of the Maxwell Communication Group of Companies.

ISBN 0-684-19627-1
ISSN 1068-9567

Printed in the United States of America

CONTENTS

·

v

Contents

vi

Contents

ACKNOWLEDGMENTS

·

My greatest appreciation goes to my assistant, Allison Diamond, my editor at Collier Books, Mark Chimsky, and Bill Rosen, the publisher of Collier/Macmillan. In addition, many thanks to my father Bill Bright, Gayle Rubin, Anne Semans, Joan Blank, David Steinberg, Brigitte and Robert Mak, matisse, Bonnie Nadel, Felice Newman, Tony Lovett, Bill Tonelli, Will Blythe, John Borrelli, Mark Pritchard, Mel Freilicher, John Preston, Lily Burana, Michele Slung, Jack Hafferkemp and Marianna Beck.

INTRODUCTION

·

In the beginning, in America, there was smut. There was no "Best American Erotica," because anything erotic was likely to be considered in the Worst Possible Taste — if it was considered at all. Like a bastard that everyone knows but no one acknowledges, erotica has had a rich life in American folk culture, humor, and songs; never published except surreptitiously, never criticized except in jest.

I asked my father once, "What was the first 'dirty' story you ever saw?" He remembered that when he was a schoolboy in the 1930s, he came into possession of a page of rhyme typewritten on carbon copies and passed around the playground. This was typical enough — forty years later, I was sneaking my first look at a "fuck book" that was passed through the eighth grade locker room. The only thing that changed was the carbon copies. Erotica was not printed by any respectable American press nor was it sold in ordinary bookstores until the early sixties.

Our erotic writing has lived like this, in a ghetto of prurient interest, a segregated twilight world with many class and racial boundaries. Until the last three decades, its pleasures and initiatives were largely reserved for men.

Sexual repression is not simply about words and pictures. Everywhere that erotic art has been suppressed, sexual behavior is similarly curtailed. In any state where laws prevent adults from consensual relations, there too, the harshest censorship prevails. In Georgia, for example, not only are you forbidden from performing a cozy act of sodomy in the privacy of your own home, you are also barred from buying or selling pictures of such sinful deeds; and you would have a hard time even reading about such subjects.

It's not just the South where we see these broad definitions of obscenity; it's all over the United States, in any region where a strong religious tradition prevails over a population that experiences little change.

Our Puritan founders were not known for bringing enlightened erotic beliefs across the Atlantic. More than any other nation that preceded it, the United States was founded on a punitive sense of sexuality. Immigrants, natives, and slaves who were subsequently conquered/assimilated were each given a walloping dose of Anglo-Saxon prudery. The American world of arts and letters came of age under such morality and double standards.

When erotica has not been directly banned, it has been

derided. It wasn't that long ago that Erica Jong was called a "mammoth pudenda" by *The New Statesman* for her break-through novel, *Fear of Flying,* the first contemporary women's erotic novel. In a different world, I would like to think such a title would be the highest compliment.

Sexual fiction has traditionally been ridiculed for lack of intellectual substance or eloquence, and for its commerciality or dehumanizing qualities. But are these doubts based on our personal feeling about sex? Are we bored by desire, immune to lust, objectified by passion? Hardly.

This first volume of *Best American Erotica* is an unprece-dented collection of outstanding erotic literature. It is worth reviewing the history of sexual politics in America to un-derstand why such a volume of stories can exist today when it would have been impossible even five years ago. The bad name given to erotica is a direct result of chauvinism, sexual repression, and its big stick, the legal arm of censorship.

The history of literary censorship in the United States is a history of erotic silence. When the Bill of Rights was com-posed, its authors had no clue that the First Amendment would be most sorely tested not by partisan dissent, or abolition, or suffrage, but by explicit sexual speech. Think of D. H. Lawrence's *Lady Chatterley's Lover,* first printed in Italy in 1928. Of course Lawrence was not Italian — his work was considered too sexually explicit to be printed in England or the United States at the time. How about Rad-clyffe Hall's *Well of Loneliness,* written in the twenties? It wasn't even erotic, but the mere acknowledgment of lesbi-anism was considered obscene. And in the greatest *cause célèbre* of obscenity cases, one of our greatest writers, Henry Miller, did not see his milestone *Tropic of Cancer* available legally in the United States until twenty-seven years after he published it in Paris. I remember my parents smuggled home a paperback copy of it on their return from Europe in the fifties.

They weren't the only ones. In those days, hundreds of American readers passed around underground copies of Miller's soliloquies on the "Land of Fuck" that he described so vividly in *Tropic of Cancer*, *Tropic of Capricorn*, and *Black Spring*. Among those smitten were the heralds of the Beat Generation: Burroughs, Di Prima, Ginsberg, Kerouac, and later, on the West Coast, Bukowski. Miller's tradition of declaring the insistence and prerogative of a masculine desire can be seen in erotic writers ever since, even in contemporary settings such as Michael Dorsey's "Milk" or Ronald Sukenick's "The Flood" in this collection.

Obviously the development of erotic writing has suffered from stagnation in a quasi-legal atmosphere. Can we imagine what quality we would find in mystery novels if such writing was banned? When subjects are not spoken about, criticized, or appreciated openly, they stay the same; their readers are reduced to the habits of shock value and predictable titillation.

The perfect example of the sexually illiterate rut we're in is our vocabulary: Erotica and Pornography. That's it. Two words, and the tiresome debate over what each stands for. Always a symbol of class difference, "erotica" and "pornography" are like neighborhoods that don't think much of each other, and it's obvious who lives on the wrong side of the tracks.

Pornography is usually called out as a put-down, except when people want to insinuate just how down-and-dirty exciting their subject is. *Erotica* is usually used as a compliment, except when it's delivered with sarcasm from the skeptic who doesn't believe that anything hanging in a museum could turn anyone on.

At its worst, the label of pornography is a trick; cheap or expensive, but a con all the same. It says, "I know your sordid guilty secret, now pay up and get out."

At its best, pornography is a dead-honest hard-on, the blush spreading across the breast. Despite pornography's animated parade of stereotypes and predictable taboos, it tells no lie. It is like the ultimate four-letter word that accepts no substitutes.

Erotica, at its worst, is pretentious and trite, with or without the politically correct afterglow. It's snobbish, yet transparent. It won't scare the horses, but by the same token, it doesn't transport you at all. Yet at its very best, erotica is a sensual and sexual aesthetic with a mind of its own. It is the only concept, however fragile, that gives consideration to sex as art.

From this artistic viewpoint, music, theater, and film were all revolutionized by the sexual frankness that characterized the 1960s. The candor pioneered by beat writers of the preceding decade influenced the mainstream in novels as commercial as *Valley of the Dolls*.

Meanwhile the underground integrated their sexual and

erotic discussions into a "political equals personal" revolution. Feminists analyzed the myth of the vaginal orgasm and urged women to leave the virgin/whore mentality in the dust. My own generation regarded masturbation as an act of self-determination as well as pleasure.

While feminists explored the territory of sexual entitlement, gay male authors writing for small presses in the 1970s raised the profound question of sexual identity in literature. Both groups rejected the notion that diverse sexual expression was necessarily built on a foundation of guilt and neuroses. The walls were coming down.

Despite its debatable reputation for prudery, feminism has been the most fertile wellspring for modern erotic writing of our times. When women announced, "My body belongs to me," they not only took physical territory, they liberated the female gaze. How did women feel about their bodies? What did good girls really think about sex, and who were the bad girls, anyway? Feminists may have started off talking about the clitoris, but it wasn't long before discussion turned to the most erotic part of the body: the mind. Author Nancy Friday inadvertently published the most popular erotic literature of the seventies, *My Secret Garden* and *Forbidden Flowers*, a survey of women's erotic fantasies. She followed with a group of men revealing the same taboos and secrets. The lid of Pandora's box was blown off for good.

Women's erotica has been most forceful in two directions. One is the dissolving of stereotypes, the embrace of a wildly diverse female sexuality. The other factor has been a quality in women's fiction I call femmchismo.

Femmchismo is the aggressive, seductive and very hungry sexual ego of a woman. Certainly the stereotype of a female predator is not new: the spider, the manipulator, the schemer. Her sexual wiles are designed to procure something other than sex. What's new is that now, when women describe their sexual courage and pride, their erotic satisfaction is their explicit goal, to be sexually adventurous for her own sake!

I wrote this explanation in *Herotica 2,* one of a series of women's erotic fiction anthologies that debuted in the eighties after similar ground-breaking collections appeared from editor/sex therapist Lonnie Barbach.

As co-editor of *Herotica 2* with Joan Blank, I was fascinated with how successful the book was and how many of its authors were publishing for the first time. My favorite selections particularly pointed to women who were breaking the back of clichés. In "Rubenesque," an independent woman with an ample figure enjoys a scandalous episode in her local ritzy hotel, with impeccable consciousness of her body from the first sentence to the last. In "Ellen, from Chicago," we have the story of how a lesbian relationship develops between two black civil rights workers on the road together in the South during the early sixties.

What both stories share is strongly drawn women characters, with a depth and individuality unheard of in Hollywood formulas. Like other stories in this collection, such as Anita "Melissa" Mashman's "Five Dimes" or Anne Marie Mardith's "Serenade for Female with Fantasies," they articulate an honest female sexual response, absolutely unheard of in a Harlequin-style romance.

Femmchismo is sometimes as simple as a woman taking a chance, doing something that only a man would do, except that since she's a woman, it turns out differently. Look at Blake Aaren's "I Have Something for You," where a lesbian lover marches into uncharted butch territory with her girlfriend, or "Ninety-Three Million Miles Away," where Barbara Gowdy's heroine pursues an unusual exhibitionist/voyeur relationship.

The other underground influence that has had a powerful effect on erotica has been gay men's literature — although this is changing as gay life becomes a more common topic in all types of publishing. But it's fair to say that gay erotica has always been more discriminating than straight, in pictures as well as words. John Rechy wrote eloquently and explicitly about hustling in Grove Press's *Evergreen Review* in 1958, where his novel *City of Night* was first serialized. *Evergreen* was exceptional, but even the stupidest gay brown paper wrapper often has an element of craft or character to it that would not be found in its heterosexual counterpart. No straight "skin mag" regularly publishes first-rate erotic fiction, but that is exactly what one could expect to find reading any of the popular gay sex magazines, be it *Drummer* or *Honcho* or *Advocate Men*.

Two of the pieces in this volume originally appeared in the kind of magazines that don't get listed on anybody's resumé: purchased on the shelf in the back of the cigar store. Their appearance here is thanks to one of the most talented and prolific "gay porn" writers and editors, John Preston, who made history in 1978 with his erotic leatherman's novel,

Mr. Benson, serialized in *Drummer.* Last year, Preston compiled the best of contemporary gay erotica, like Leigh Rutledge's "Brian's Bedroom" and Pat Califia's "Belonging," rescuing them from years of obscurity by putting them into a collection called *Flesh and the Word,* and helping them reach a "legitimate" bookstore audience for the first time.

Pat Califia is one of the few women ever to have erotic stories featured in a gay men's magazine. She first wrote about lesbian S/M and gender-bending when such topics were anathema to the lesbian establishment. She is the perfect example of how radical women, and lesbians in particular, have transformed the understanding of S/M and gender roles in erotic publishing.

Califia, whether in her own words or as inspiration, was central to a lesbian sex tidal wave of small press books and magazines of the eighties, with such telling names as *Coming to Power, On Our Backs, Bad Attitude,* and *Outrageous Women.* Califia's own short story collection, *Macho Sluts,* was the perfect title that defined the new lesbian sex genre: irreverent, arresting, and unapologetically pornographic.

I remember the first American Booksellers Association convention I attended in 1986 in Washington, D.C.; I was the editor of *On Our Backs* at the time. A New York publisher took one look at my magazine and said, "I thought lesbian sex was a contradiction in terms!" Well, think again, buddy. *Best American Erotica* wouldn't be here today if it weren't for the desktop revolution in lesbian and women's writing.

It was also a woman writer, Anne Rice, who brought homoeroticism onto the bestseller lists. It would be hard to imagine any erotica treasury that didn't include her work. As the originator of the most compelling Vampire legend since Dracula, Rice brought explicit eroticism to her first books about her vampire-hero, Lestat, as well as her other novels about ante-bellum life in New Orleans (*The Feast of All Saints*) and the history of Castrato singers in eighteenth-century Italy (*Cry to Heaven*).

Rice applied her talent as a romantic writer to explore male homosexuality in her novels as unselfconsciously as her characters drew a breath. New writers like Carol Queen, represented here by "Golden Boy," or Trish Thomas, upping the ante in "Me and the Boys," have taken the notion of genderfuck and run with them. But Rice was the first to make this mark. She is still the only author who can turn a historical romantic novel upside-down with a feminine articulation of gay sex.

This unique treatment on Rice's part was nothing compared to her next move. In the mid-eighties Rice pseudonymously published the *Beauty* series, a trio of novels (*The Claiming of Sleeping Beauty, Beauty's Punishment, Beauty's Release*) dripping with Victorian/fairytale sado-masochism. Rice delighted in composing the most riveting one-handed reading since *The Story of O*. The *Beauty* series was unabashedly arousing, transcending boundaries of gender and sexual preference, and providing a radical reply to the ideas that a woman or a feminist would never write about extremes of sexual desire.

Are women better erotic writers than men? How can this make any kind of sense? Women are not naturally more adept at eroticism, and they are certainly less experienced than male authors in charting erotic territory.

It is precisely this lack of background, this "new kid on the block" persona, that has made women writers and editors more forthcoming. They believe erotica should be displayed and discussed with distinction. You see, women were never included in the Faustian bargain that men had, privately enjoying erotica/pornography, away from the family and kids. Men accepted the clandestine third-rate status of sexual entertainment, but women consumers never even had the opportunity to get accustomed to it. I remember when I first started working in a feminist sex-toy shop, the women customers expected their new vibrator to last like a Maytag. They didn't understand why there weren't shelves of books devoted to women's erotica. I handed them Anaïs Nin's *Delta of Venus* stories from the 1930s and said, "Sorry, this is IT." They were appalled, and rightly so. The newly liberated female erotic connoisseur was *not* content.

Some best-selling male authors have been famous for bringing their powers of observation to sexual description: Phillip Roth, Terry Southern, John Updike, and Gay Talese. Each was a one-man ticket to the essence of the male psyche arising from the sixties' sexual revolution.

The first male author to break with standard masculine conventions regarding straight sex was Nicholson Baker in his novel *Vox*. Its simple premise, a revealing phone sex conversation between two people linked by thousands of optic fibers, constituted the first virtual erotica. Phone sex itself, which has had all the cachet of a knock-knock joke, was transformed in his novel into a most revealing picture of a man and a woman sharing their souls as simultaneously as they parted their lips.

Baker's departure from the norm is that he portrays the woman character's point of view as convincingly as the man's. Her secrets are delivered from honest feminine knowledge. The man's vulnerability is entwined with his virility, rather than posed as its undoing.

Of course, readers expect a skilled writer to compose experiences from all walks of life. But in ghettoizing erotica, we have thought that only men could portray male sexuality realistically, and that only women could speak authentically about their own desires. Gay and straight sensibilities have been similarly strait-jacketed. From Rice to Califia to Baker there has come one answer to that tight-fitting cliché: NOT.

Rice and Baker are best-selling authors, and both have taken their share of criticism for lacking seriousness because their work embraced sex. Excerpts from their recent novels, *The Tale of the Body Thief* and *Vox*, respectively, are included here.

Two other widely read authors in *Best American Erotica* this year are Robert Silverberg and Samuel R. Delany, both distinguished science fiction writers. Interestingly, erotica is given a bit more respect in the science fiction world, perhaps because sci-fi itself was also once a bastard child of literature, unavailable at public libraries or proper book shops. It's no coincidence that one of the most successful publishers of erotica, *Penthouse,* is also the publisher of the futuristic magazine *OMNI.*

Popular culture seems to inevitably shake the shoulders of the establishment, saying, "Listen, wake up!" At the same time that erotic work is viewed dimly by the established art world, it manages to make its way under everyone's bedcovers. The hypocrisy becomes unbearable. Truth seekers point out that not only isn't the Emperor wearing any clothes; he's also in the middle of an orgy.

I reviewed a manuscript for this collection from a novel that was about to be excerpted in a major men's magazine. The story opens with a couple who can't keep their hands off each other coming home from the airport in a cab. It was very well drawn, the characters promising, begging for an orgasmic climax. The taxi scene was cut short after a few pages, and this left me breathless. I silently congratulated the writers for teasing me into a delirium, and I gnawed through the next chapter searching for relief. It never came. I felt like the storyteller was sticking his tongue out at me, saying, "See, I could write erotica if I wanted to, but I won't because it's beneath me as a master of fine literature."

Actually I doubt that the author was intending to send such a personal telegraph, but this example of aborting an erotic scene is common to the point of banality. What gets called good taste is actually the process of reducing finely built erotic preludes into gratuitous titillation, thereby avoiding the power of sexual description.

Because mainstream publishing has been so reluctant to explore sex, few authors have bucked the trend of self-

censorship and erotic avoidance. It has been small presses
and underground periodicals that have mined the treasure
of modern erotic writing. Only recently, a few rebellious
academic journals have taken on the risks of polymorphous
perversity; this is exactly where I found such wonderful work
for this collection as Ronald Sukenick's "The Flood" and an
excerpt from Samuel Delany's forthcoming novel *Citre et
Trans*. Alternative journals like *Frighten the Horses* or academic
ones like *Fiction International* don't worry on a grand scale
about sales being lost, bookstores canceling, fundamentalists
protesting — because these publishers and their readers in-
habit a different world.

This new world can no longer be called a twilight zone
because it is a triumph of counter-culture, a world of art and
ideas so influential that the mainstream can't help but keep
an eye on it. Lily Burana, the editor of *Taste of Latex* magazine, has a name for the material she publishes: Entertainment for the "Differently-Interested." But that's the point —
we *all* have different interests.

As erotica has mirrored changing political times, it has
reflected the state and health of our bodies in the nineties.
AIDS and subsequent safer sex practices have raised tremendous controversy in the sexual entertainment industry.
Many people have raised "safe sex" visibility as a sort of
seat-belt directive for erotic artists.

But if writers feel any duty to their work, it is to deliver
both the brutal truth and the most far-flung fantasy. Neither
case has anything to do with including labels and warnings
as if fiction was product advertising. Safer sex practices have

inevitably become a part of erotic fiction, if only because risk itself is an indelible part of sexuality. The panic of lust, the burden of obstacles, and the attraction to denial in sexual relations is an unbeatable aphrodisiac. Nostalgia, as in Carter Wilson's "In Griff's in L.A. on a Rainy Sunday Afternoon in February," describes the tug and drift of by-gone days, another feature of post-plague eroticism. It's no longer the Summer of '42 we rhapsodize; it's the end of 1979 and risk as we knew it.

Despite the recent changing of the guard in American politics, a conservative bully pulpit has dominated public policy for so long that it was inevitable that erotic writing would take a satiric and even rant-like twist. In "Horny," Greg Boyd takes below-the-belt evangelical zeal and makes it come alive in a wicked cross-section of the sacrilegious and libidinous. Lisa Palac's "Needless to Say" has a John Waters–inspired sense of subversion as a porn star wanna-be takes over her local supermart. Sue Bob says check it out.

But other writers have no patience left for anything but a frontal assault. In "Me and the Boys," Trish Thomas takes the Kinsey Scale and jams it in the blender. In Bob Flanagan's "WHY:," the author is in our face with his sexual affront, telling us to dig it or dig our own grave. His politics of outrage are as apparent as his poignant memories of everything from fairy tales to fetishes to childhood lessons learned in a hospital bed. Confrontational erotica like this takes the sensuality of pain, the impact of a nuclear (as in explosive) family, plus the indignation of being ignored, and wraps it up into one tight missile.

✿   ✿   ✿

When I told a friend that I was writing the introduction to the very first *Best American Erotica*, he laughed at my great seriousness: "All people want to know is whether they are supposed to get off on it or not."

"Well, of course they are," I said. "It would be a gigantic failure if they read the whole book and didn't find one thing that moved them to a bit of ecstasy."

I didn't like his bottom line. "Listen," I said, "This is a group of writers who aren't content to hold the reader by the balls or by the tip of their clit. They are people who have something to say about the world, about human nature, about our oldest secrets and greatest mysteries."

We learn from erotica, just like a lover learns from touch, from tasting, from the greatest teacher of all, sex. I tell my friend, you may not ignite with each of these stories, but you can't help but feel the fire.

Susie Bright
SAN FRANCISCO   1993

THE
BEST
AMERICAN
EROTICA
1993

RUBENESQUE

Magenta Michaels

•

It was nearly noon when "The Mountain," as she was known
to her slimmer and catty co-workers, left the confines of her
eighth-floor accounting office, hailed a cab, and within ten
minutes alighted at the entrance of the grand and formidable
Clift Hotel.

Actually, Evie Satterwhite wasn't really a mountain anymore; these days she more resembled a sweetly sloping knoll,
resulting from many months of diminished intake and nearly
5,000 miles on her stationary bike. And while many women
still dismissed her as heavy and in need of a good diet, many
men looked at Evie and figuratively licked their lips, finding
her rounded good looks toothsome and much preferable to
the brittle edges of her slimmer sisters. Evie was not unaware
of her effect on such men and helped it along. No drab power

suits with skinny neckties for her but rather glossed red lips, high-heeled sandals showing off gorgeously arched feet, and softly glowing hair — colored Titian Red — that she fluffed with perfectly manicured fingertips. Men dropped like flies.

And so, in small celebration of her growing self-confidence and her diminishing heft, she came each month for lunch at this fabulous hotel where, for the price of many lunches at Alex's Deli next door to the office, she joined society ladies and literary buffs who assembled to hear the authors of famous and infamous bestsellers discuss their work. And, for the price of the same ticket, have an exquisitely catered, designer lunch.

Once in the lobby, she found her way to The Redwood Room, a draped and muraled splendor heavy with tapestries and chandeliers. She was the first to arrive and the room was empty, though each of the fifty tables in the hall was wonderfully appointed with heavy pink table linen and flowers at every place, silverware and wineglasses gleaming under the lights of the chandeliers. Evie stood in the doorway for a long time deciding where she would sit, and it was then that she saw the two workmen tacking down a portion of the richly patterned carpet. They looked up when she stepped through the polished double doors, and one of them — small and trim with Mediterranean good looks — immediately smiled at her and sat back on his heels, his eyes gobbling up the bounce of her hips as she passed him. She chose one of the smaller tables with two upholstered chairs and a loveseat, set against a side wall. And while the table was not near the lectern, from there she could see everyone who entered with-

out having to turn around to look. She settled herself,
checked her watch and was immediately distracted by the
arrival of a noisy group of fashionably dressed matrons; fur
coats, reptile skins, and expensive perfume ruffled the air
around her as they passed. Slowly the room filled, and at
12:45 jacketed waiters began to serve. Her plate was set
before her: a gorgeous, spa-inspired creation of poached
salmon resting on a technicolor bed of various perfect greens
and raw vegetables. Freshly baked bread lay steaming in a
cloth basket, and even before she could think to ask, her
wine was being poured by her silent but attentive waiter.

From the corner of her eye she saw, still on his knees
and very near her table, the carpet man gathering his things
to go. Then, with mounting disbelief, she watched him gaze
intently at her, look carefully around him, lift the corner of
her tablecloth, and quickly disappear, crawling beneath its
skirts. Riveted, she stared wide-eyed at her wineglass, its
amber contents trembling and then sloshing with the movements of the table as the man settled himself underneath it.
Glancing at her neighbors to see who might have witnessed
this phenomenon, she found herself unobserved. Not knowing what else to do, she fumbled in the bread basket for the
miniature loaf, broke off a tiny piece and nervously began
to butter it. Somehow feeling this was not the appropriate
thing to do, she lay the bread down and picked up the heavy
silver fork, fluffing the salad greens on her plate. The man
beneath her table had not moved.

Of course she fully expected him to come crawling out
at any moment, confused, flushed, and apologetic, and she,

in her excited mind's eye, would smile sympathetically and nod him away, glancing around the room at the other diners who by now would all be staring. They would shrug their shoulders ("These things *do* happen") and then turn their interests back to their exquisitely detailed lunches or the brilliant wit of the speaker who was about to take the lectern. So she waited, gleaming fork poised above the burst of colors on her plate.

But he didn't come out and he didn't move, continuing to kneel there, his breath an intermittent warming to her knees. Through the haze of her growing excitement the oddest array of thoughts possessed her: could he *see* under there? Suppose the waiter spies the tablecloth moving and drags the man out by the scruff of his neck and then calls the police? Suppose the speaker at the lectern sees his feet sticking out, stops in mid-sentence, and points, as all of the diners turn around and stare at her? Suppose . . .

And then he touched her, his hands encircling the shoe of her crossed leg, causing her to start with such violence that her fork clattered heavily to the plate, scattering bits of salmon and vegetables onto the pink tablecloth between the porcelain cups and half-filled, beveled wineglasses. Dazed, she collected bits of food and placed them on the corner of her plate. Broad, warm fingers stroked the leather of her heeled sandal and the nylon at the top of her foot, the tiny rough places on the surface of his hands catching at the silken finish of her sheer stocking. He held her foot motionless for the longest time, and when she did not move or protest, he carefully removed her shoe, slipping it off with one hand and

4

enclosing her foot immediately with the other hand as though he wished to make certain that she remained warm and secure. Then slowly, slowly, he began to knead the arch of her foot, moving his fingers up to the ball and then to the toes. And when still she did not respond, he began to pull gently at each toe, separating and finally rubbing into the crevices between them as much as the nylon stocking would allow. Above the table, the waiter took her plate, Evie gazing at him through dreamy, unseeing eyes.

She could feel the tiny tremors of his cramped position as his mouth bent to the inside of her arch. Caressing more with teeth and tongue than with lips, he moved along the whole inside of her foot, moving his attentions slowly up to her toes, nibbling at her longer, second toe before sucking its tip deeply into his mouth. With bites and tiny caressing sucks, he made a warm, wet trail up the length of her leg from ankle to inner knee.

A rising panic made her feel that she must move her body, that if she did not she would be unable to breathe or that she might fling herself wildly from the table. To calm herself she carefully drew her foot from his hand, uncrossing her leg and changing her position on the loveseat until she was comfortable again. He, unsure of her movements, waited until she was still again before resting his forehead against her knees. Then he wriggled his head from side to side to part her legs. She could feel the roughness of his stubble, the prominent outline of nose and cheekbones as he burrowed his face against her. She allowed his head to part her as in slow motion she watched her waiter pour more coffee, the speaker at the lectern animated but voiceless for her. "Adventure," she thought dumbly. "This is what they call an adventure," as he nuzzled his way up and up with tiny bites and little licks done with the inside of his lips, alternating between her thighs, nudging her legs farther apart. As he approached her mid-thigh, she knew that he could smell her — that the smell of saliva-stroked skin, wet nylons, and her perfume mingled with the beckoning steam from between her legs, and that it rose to his nostrils as surely as the steam from her coffee floated to her own.

Abruptly the warmth of his mouth withdrew, startling her and leaving the spots where his mouth had been feeling cold and somehow desolate. During this long instant when she felt nothing from him, she began to be afraid. Then, with the purpose and familiarity of a longtime lover, he lifted his hands from her ankles and slid them, in one smooth movement, up the outer sides of her legs, pausing only at the hem of her skirt to gauge its tightness, then swept them underneath to her hips, one warm palm on each fleshy pad. He tugged at her pantyhose and she found herself helping him, shifting her weight from one buttock to the other. He slid her skirt up and up until it was bunched up around her hips, barely hidden from view by tablecloth, napkin, jacket, and the arms of the little loveseat. When he'd finally stripped the nylon from her legs, she sighed almost audibly as though some great weight had been lifted from her body. For a moment he did not touch her, and she knew that he was looking at her, inspecting her, admiring her. It added to her excitement that he could not watch the play of emotions on her face, or that she could not control him or guide him or wiggle or thrust herself up to his lips. She was at once helpless and in total control, able to take all that he was offering without guilt or reciprocation but at the same time unable to move toward him. This last thought made her smile, because should her covering table be somehow snatched away, there she would be, skirt to her waist, legs agape, a strange man with a bag of carpet tools by his side having his way with her.

When he could get no further because of her seated position, he guided her bare right foot to the seat of one of the upholstered chairs tucked under the table, spreading her legs further to allow him room. He pressed his nose against the swatch of silk that covered her crotch, rubbing up and down on either side of the distended kernel that pressed against her panties. He put his mouth to it, breathing on it, blowing at it, and finally pressing it, circling it through her panties with the tip of his tongue. She had all but stopped breathing, the room forgotten, the speaker's voice a senseless drone. Then, with one finger, he hooked the edge of her panties and drew them to one side, and dragged his tongue in one long velvet stroke from the base of her asshole to the top of her swollen clitoris.

"More coffee, madam?" The waiter bent to her ear. She looked up at him, unable to answer as the man beneath the table worked away, massaging her outer lips between his teeth, curling his tongue in her hair, pressing, blowing, sucking time and again the little kernel of flesh. Release rose up in her, washing over her limbs like smoke, and he held her stiffened legs pressed against his sides as she covered her face with the linen napkin, pressing it to her eyes to cover her grimace. Everyone in the room was clapping, the sound coming through to her consciousness like the volume on a TV crowd scene being quickly turned up and then down. Were they applauding her? Him? The speaker?

She opened her eyes to diners, rising to go. The luncheon was over. Crumpled and exhausted she sat at her table until the room was nearly empty. He had knelt back, no longer touching her, and she knew it was time for her to decide what to do. Awkwardly, she lowered her skirts, arranging her jacket and removing her foot from the chair. Feeling with one foot, she found her shoe and swung her legs to the side to slip into it. She pushed the table back slightly and rose to go, her legs wobbly, her head light. As she stepped across the doorway, she looked back at the table, its cluttered surface and pink skirts looking for all the world like the fifty others in the room. It looked as though nothing had happened here except a lecture and a luncheon and she was tempted to go back, to raise the tablecloth to see if he indeed was still crouched underneath.

No, she would not go back. She would not look under, or wait for him to come out and approach her. Maybe it was a dream. But as she stepped out toward the main lobby a woman in a fur coat whispered loudly to her companion, "I thought bare legs were only acceptable on thin French mannequins!" And Evie, looking down at her stockingless legs, smiled as she remembered her rumpled pair of damp nylons lying under the table. Queen size.

from
THE TALE OF
THE BODY THIEF
THE VAMPIRE CHRONICLES

Anne Rice

•

(Editor's note: *Lestat is an ancient vampire who finds himself tasting contemporary sexuality for the first time in centuries when he makes a deal to temporarily "trade" bodies with a handsome American mortal.*)

Well, it was perfectly obvious which marvelous human experience was meant to come now. But I could feel nothing for her. Nothing. I smiled, and I began to take off my clothes. I peeled off the overcoat, and was immediately cold. Why wasn't she cold? I then took off the sweater and was immediately horrified by the smell of my own sweat. *Lord God, was it really like this before?* And this body of mine had looked so clean.

She didn't seem to notice. I was grateful for that. I then

removed my shirt and my shoes and my socks and my pants. My feet were still cold. Indeed, I was cold and naked, very naked. I didn't know whether or not I liked this at all. I suddenly saw myself in the mirror over her dressing table, and I realized that this organ was of course utterly drunk and asleep.

Again, she didn't seem surprised.

"Come here," she said. "Sit down."

I obeyed. I was shivering all over. Then I began to cough. The first cough was a spasm, catching me completely by surprise. Then a whole series of coughs followed, uncontrollably, and the last was so violent that it made a circle of pain around my ribs.

"I'm sorry," I said to her.

"I love your French accent," she whispered. She stroked my hair, and let her nails lightly scratch my cheek.

Now, this was a pleasant sensation. I bent my head and kissed her throat. Yes, this was nice also. It was nothing as exciting as closing on a victim, but it was nice. I tried to remember what it had been like two hundred years ago when I was the terror of the village girls. Seems some farmer was always at the castle gates, cursing me and swinging his fist at me and telling me that if his daughter was with child by me, I'd have to do something about it! It had all seemed such wonderful fun at the time. And the girls, oh the lovely girls.

"What is it?" she asked.

"Nothing," I said. I kissed her throat again. I could smell sweat on her body too. I didn't like it. But why? These smells were nothing as sharp, any of them, as they were to me in my other body. But they connected with something in this body — that was the ugly part. I felt no protection against these smells; they seemed not artifacts but something which could invade me and contaminate me. For instance, the sweat from her neck was now on my lips. I knew it was, I could taste it and I wanted to be away from her.

Ah, but this is madness. She was a human being, and I was a human being. Thank God this would be over Friday. But what right had I to thank God!

Her little nipples brushed against my chest, very hot and nubby and the flesh behind them was squashy and tender. I slipped my arm around her small back.

"You're hot, I think you have a fever," she said in my ear. She kissed my neck the way I'd been kissing hers.

"No, I'm all right," I said. But I didn't have the slightest idea of whether or not this was true. This was hard work!

Suddenly her hand touched my organ, startling me, and then bringing about an immediate sensation. I felt the organ lengthen and grow hard. The sensation was entirely concentrated, and yet it galvanized me. When I looked at her breasts now, and down at the small fur triangle between her legs, my organ grew even more hard. Yes, I remember this all right; my eyes are connected to it, and nothing else matters now, hmmm, all right. Just get her down on the bed.

"Whoa!" she whispered. "Now that's a piece of equipment!"

"Is it?" I looked down. The monstrous thing had doubled

11

in size. It did seem grossly out of proportion to everything else. "Yes, I suppose it is. Should have known James would have checked it out."

"Who's James?"

"No, doesn't matter," I mumbled. I turned her face towards me and kissed her wet little mouth this time, feeling her teeth through her thin lips. She opened her mouth for my tongue. This was good, even if her mouth was bad tasting. Didn't matter. But then my mind raced ahead to blood. Drink her blood.

Where was the pounding intensity of drawing near the victim, of the moment right before my teeth pierced the skin and the blood spilled all over my tongue?

No, it's not going to be that easy, or that consuming. It's going to go between the legs and more like a shiver, but this is some shiver, I'll say that.

Merely thinking of the blood had heightened the passion, and I shoved her roughly down on the bed. I wanted to finish, nothing else mattered but finishing.

"Wait a minute," she said.

"Wait for what?" I mounted her, and kissed her again, pushing my tongue deeper into her. No blood. Ah, so pale. No blood. My organ slid between her hot thighs, and I almost spurted then. But it wasn't enough.

"I said wait!" she screamed, her cheeks coloring. "You can't do it without a condom."

"What the hell are you saying?" I murmured. I knew the meaning of these words, yet they didn't make much sense.

I pushed my hand down, felt the hair opening, and then the juicy wet crack, which seemed deliciously small.

She screamed at me to get off of her, and she shoved at me with the heels of her hands. She looked very flushed and beautiful to me suddenly in her heat and rage, and when she nudged me with her knee, I slammed down against her, then drew up only long enough to ram the organ into her, and feel that sweet hot tight envelope of flesh close around me, making me gasp.

"Don't! Stop it! I said stop it!" she screamed.

But I couldn't wait. What the hell made her think this was the time to discuss such a thing, I wondered, in some vague crazed fashion. Then, in a moment of blinding spasmodic excitement I came. Semen came roaring out of the organ!

One moment it was eternal; the next it was finished, as if it had never begun. I lay exhausted on top of her, drenched with sweat, of course, and faintly annoyed by the stickiness of the whole event, and her panic-stricken screams.

At last I fell over onto my back. My head was aching, and all the evil smells of the room thickened — a soiled smell from the bed itself, with its sagging, lumpy mattress; the nauseating smell of the cats.

She leapt out of the bed. She appeared to have gone mad. She was crying and shivering, and she snatched up a blanket from the chair and covered herself with it and began screaming at me to get out, get out, get out.

"Whatever is the matter with you?" I asked.

13

She let loose with a volley of modern curses. "You bum, you miserable stupid bum, you idiot, you jerk!" That sort of thing. I could have given her a disease, she said. Indeed she rattled off the names of several; I could have gotten her pregnant. I was a creep, a prick, a putz! I was to clear out of here at once. How dare I do this to her? Get out before she called the police.

A wave of sleepiness passed over me. I tried to focus upon her, in spite of the darkness. Then came a sudden nausea sharper than I'd ever felt. I struggled to keep it under control, and only by a severe act of will managed not to vomit then and there.

Finally, I sat up and then climbed to my feet. I looked down at her as she stood there, crying, and screaming at me, and I saw suddenly that she was wretched, that I had really hurt her, and indeed there was an ugly bruise on her face.

Very slowly it came clear to me what had happened. She had wanted me to use some form of prophylactic, and I'd virtually forced her. No pleasure in it for her, only fear. I saw her again at the moment of my climax, fighting me, and I realized it was utterly inconceivable to her that I could have enjoyed the struggle, enjoyed her rage and her protests, enjoyed conquering her. But in a paltry and common way, I think I had.

The whole thing seemed overwhelmingly dismal. It filled me with despair. The pleasure itself had been nothing! I can't bear this, I thought, not a moment longer. If I could have

14

reached James, I would have offered him another fortune, just to return at once. Reached James . . . I'd forgotten altogether about finding a phone.

"Listen to me, ma chère," I said. "I'm sorry. Things simply went wrong. I know. I'm sorry."

She moved to slap me but I caught her wrist easily and brought her hand down, hurting her a little.

"Get out," she said again. "Get out or I'll call the police."

"I understand what you're saying to me. It's been forever since I did it. I was clumsy. I was bad."

"You're worse than bad!" she said in a deep raw voice.

And this time she did slap me. I wasn't quick enough. I was astonished by the force of the slap, how it stung. I felt of my face where she'd hit me. What an annoying little pain. It was an insulting pain.

"Go!" she screamed again.

I put on my clothes, but it was like lifting sacks of bricks to do it. A dull shame had come over me, a feeling of such awkwardness and discomfort in the slightest gesture I made or smallest word I spoke that I wanted simply to sink into the earth.

Finally, I had everything buttoned and zipped properly, and I had the miserable wet socks on my feet again, and the thin shoes, and I was ready to go.

She sat on the bed crying, her shoulders very thin, with the tender bones in her back poking at her pale flesh, and her hair dripping down in thick wavy clumps over the blanket

15

she held to her breast. How fragile she looked—how sadly unbeautiful and repulsive.

I tried to see her as if I were really Lestat. But I couldn't do it. She appeared a common thing, utterly worthless, not even interesting. I was vaguely horrified. Had it been that way in my boyhood village? I tried to remember those girls, those girls dead and gone for centuries, but I couldn't see their faces. What I remembered was happiness, mischief, a great exuberance that had made me forget for intermittent periods the deprivation and hopelessness of my life.

What did that mean in this moment? How could this whole experience have been so unpleasant, so seemingly pointless? Had I been myself I would have found her fascinating as an insect is fascinating; even her little rooms would have appeared quaint to me, in their worst, most uninspiring details! Ah, the affection I always felt for all sad little mortal habitats. But why was that so!

And she, the poor thing, she would have been beautiful to me simply because she was alive! I could not have been sullied by her had I fed on her for an hour. As it was, I felt filthy for having been with her, and filthy for being cruel to her. I understood her fear of disease! I, too, felt contaminated! But where lay the perspective of truth?

"I am so sorry," I said again. "You must believe me. It wasn't what I wanted. I don't know what I wanted."

"You're crazy," she whispered bitterly without looking up.

"Some night I'll come to you, soon, and I'll bring you a

present, something beautiful that you really want. I'll give it to you and perhaps you'll forgive me."

She didn't answer.

"Tell me, what is it you really want? Money doesn't matter. What is it you want that you cannot have?"

She looked up, rather sullenly, her face blotched and red and swollen, and then she wiped at her nose with the back of her hand.

"You know what I wanted," she said in a harsh, disagreeable voice, which was almost sexless it was so low.

"No, I don't. Tell me what."

Her face was so disfigured and her voice so strange that she frightened me. I was still woozy from the wine I'd drunk earlier, yet my mind was unaffected by the intoxication. It seemed a lovely situation. This body drunk, but not me.

"Who are you?" she asked. She looked very hard now, hard and bitter. "You're somebody, aren't you . . . you're not just . . ." But her voice trailed off.

"You wouldn't believe me if I told you."

She turned her head even more sharply to the side, studying me as if it was all going to come to her suddenly. She'd have it figured out. I couldn't imagine what was going on in her mind. I knew only that I felt sorry for her, and I did not like her. I didn't like this dirty messy room with its low plaster ceiling, and the nasty bed, and the ugly tan carpet and the dim light and the cat box reeking in the other room.

"I'll remember you," I said miserably yet tenderly. "I'll surprise you. I'll come back and I'll bring something won-

17

derful for you, something you could never get for yourself. A gift as if from another world. But right now, I have to leave you."

"Yes," she said, "you'd better go."

I turned to do exactly that. I thought of the cold outside, of Mojo waiting in the hallway, and of the town house with its back door shattered off the hinges, and no money and no phone.

BRIAN'S BEDROOM

Leigh Rutledge

•

A pair of dirty jeans lying on the floor in the doorway to Brian's bedroom. The jeans are like an animal curled up, only pretending to be asleep. They were obviously tossed there in haste, a last-minute thought before his departure. The ass of the jeans is deeply faded and frayed: there are slashlike rips around the rear pockets, at those points where a guy's ass rubs hardest against the inside of the denim. Something about them just lying there makes me ache for a moment, the way the sight of some beautiful boy walking down the sidewalk, a shirtless boy one will never know, can make one ache — the kind of pang you forget a second after it comes and the boy is out of sight. The door to the bedroom itself is half-closed. Walking by it, I get a glimpse inside but see only shadows, indistinct shapes — a volleyball, dirty socks, and a leather belt. . . .

"He's such a slob," Dave tells me good-naturedly.

In the morning, on the way to the bathroom to take a piss, I stop for a minute and push Brian's bedroom door open slightly to look inside.

The curtains are drawn. At the foot of the bed is another pair of jeans. There are a couple of posters on the wall. A weight-lifting bench, some ski equipment, a black leather jacket, sleek and luminous, with rows of soft creases down the arms, a sign of the leather adapting to the flesh that wears it — all muted and slightly unreal in the dirty gray light, like objects floating in a dream. . . .

"What are you doing?"

I turn around. Dave is looking at me with a hesitant smile on his face.

"How long is he gone?" I ask nonchalantly.

"He won't be back until Friday. He's in Oklahoma City visiting his parents for a week. Why don't you get dressed so we can go get some breakfast? I'm famished."

Brian is Dave's new roommate. I've never met him, I've never even seen him. In fact, I've only talked to him once on the phone, briefly — a masculine, reasonably sexy voice, easy and flirtatious — the voice of a vain boy always on the lookout for admirers, or at least a good lay. He's twenty-two. Dave describes him as being incredibly hot, a real beauty: smooth, muscular, with darkish blond hair and deep-blue eyes, and "the sweetest ass you've ever seen — white, creamy, flawless." Almost sweeter than his ass, though, Dave tells me, are his lips: full, masculine, and beautifully shaped. "Hungry-looking," Dave adds with that pride, a kind of flaunting possessiveness some people exhibit just having a beautiful roommate they know everyone else desires and envies them for.

He and Brian have never had sex or anything; they're not lovers, just roommates. Dave tells me he thinks Brian is bisexual — or *was* bisexual — or is maybe just a little confused still. "He jacks off enough though," Dave tells me dispassionately. "I mean, I can hear him going at it in there every night." Dave shrugs and laughs. "It doesn't seem to bother him. At least he isn't a screamer like Lawrence was. Remember when you were here last April?"

Dave has to go in to work for an hour or so, and after he leaves, I walk in and look around Brian's bedroom, not with any specific intent, just with a kind of bored and nagging sexual curiosity. Who is this boy? What is he like? Pushing open the door all the way, I feel a strong adrenaline rush, the way I used to feel as a kid surreptitiously exploring my parents' dresser drawers or sneaking a peek at the dirty books my father always kept hidden under some old clothes at the back of his bedroom closet.

The feeling of stepping into the middle of someone else's life is strong.

The curtains are drawn against the bedroom's only window. There's a cooped-up smell of sweat and musty clothes, the evocative smell of a young male body; it's like the smell of a boy's locker room but not quite as pungent.

I walk around a volleyball in the middle of the floor and a wrinkled pair of lime-green gym shorts just beyond it. Brian seems to have left only a minute earlier. Against the right-hand wall is a weight-lifting bench, celebrating the body with incline bench presses, two-arm dumbbell curls, and leg pull-ins — the body as sex tool, as cultural weapon, as political statement. A stack of round weights sits in the corner, along with a wadded-up jockstrap and a scuffed pair of cross-trainers coming apart at the seams. I run my hand along the red vinyl bench and imagine some beautiful boy stripped to his jock and working out hard, with sweat on his neck, pecs, and face; his bare ass slides back and forth along the vinyl as he pumps his muscles. Maybe he jacks off sometimes after a workout, and the cum and the sweat mix in a small pool on his upper belly. He uses the jockstrap as a cum-rag, the fabric stiff and potent from semen and sweat. . . .

There are several items taped to the wall above the bench. A postcard: "Brian, Having a helluva good time (2 cut, 1 uncut). San Diego is HOT. Surfers and sailors everywhere. Flying on to SF tomorrow. Stroke it once for me, buddy — Jeff." Next to that, torn from some newspaper, a photograph of two high school wrestlers, one holding the other down on his stomach, both boys obviously struggling, obviously straining their muscles to the limit; the boy on the bottom has a harrowing and somehow intensely erotic grimace on his face, the kind of wrenched-up face you see on a young

male who is being fucked, hard, up the ass, and for whom
the feeling is both brutally shocking and a sudden revelation
of fulfillment. Next to that, a magazine photo of a shirtless
construction worker, his powerful torso sunburned, his low-
riding 501s dirty and bulging; it's an ad for a national brand
of home insurance.

My eyes scan the top of Brian's nightstand. A comb, a
cigarette lighter, a rawhide strap. There's also an ashtray,
pilfered from some casino in Las Vegas (in it are the remains
of a joint), a gray bandanna-type handkerchief rolled into a
ball, and a beaten-up paperback copy of Tom Clancy's *The
Hunt for Red October.* Sticking up out of the nightstand drawer
is part of an envelope; the return address is from Oklahoma.

Beneath the nightstand is a tall stack of porno magazines.
There are the usual gay slicks — "Rock-Hard Nudes!" "Siz-
zling Summer Fiction!" "Fraternity Flesh Issue!" "True Experiences: Our Readers Tell All!" — plus a few bondage and
S&M magazines at the very bottom, as if Brian has occasional, hesitant fantasies about kinky sex he isn't willing yet
to fess up to. There are also a couple issues of *Penthouse* and
Playboy.

As I thumb through one of the *Playboys,* a Polaroid snapshot falls out from between the pages and lands on my shoe.
It's of a tall, broad-shouldered blond boy standing naked;
he's smiling devilishly at the camera and holding a huge hard-
on toward the lens. Whoever it is — Brian or someone else —
has an enormous cock and huge balls. His hair is all di-
sheveled and standing up in the back, as if he had just come
from an active round of sex and the lingering traces of grease

and sweat in his scalp made the hair stiff and unruly. On the back of the picture someone has written, "Great fun, huh? Love, R."

Browsing through some of the jack-off magazines, I wonder which ones give Brian the biggest hard-ons, which images turn him on the most, which of these pictures — the young blond ranch hand tied to a fence post to get fucked, the sergeant licking the buck private's ass, the football player in his jockstrap and pads — does he go back to, time and time again, for the most intense and satisfying orgasms? Which of these situations and fantasies, if any, most accurately reflect his deepest longings, the sexual yearnings of an indecisively bisexual, twenty-two-year-old male? Or does he swing back and forth between *Penthouse* and the gay slicks, between fuckable women and beautiful boys, building himself up — from one kind of fuckable hole to the other — to a deep messy masculine orgasm that embraces all indiscretions, all combinations, all possibilities. . . .

It suddenly seems as if someone is in the room with me, and for a moment I look up, startled. But — no one is there. The blood vessels in my head pound for a second with a sudden, brief charge of anxiety.

There's a pair of crumpled white briefs half buried between the bedsheets. I pull them out. Jockeys. Waist 28. I raise them to my nose: the white cotton pouch smells of fabric softener and piss. Turning them over in my hands I think of what Dave said about Brian's ass: "white, creamy, flawless." My bewilderment is like touching an autograph in a book, knowing that someone has once been there, where

24

your hand is now, but at a different time. God, how I'd love to have that ass here right now. . . .

Suddenly there are unmistakable noises downstairs — Dave must be home for lunch. I shove the briefs back down between the sheets and get up from the bed.

Leaving the room is like being forced to pull my hard cock away from a warm, pleasing mouth, just when I'm about to come. . . .

Driving round town with Dave (a cursory stab at sight-seeing, even though I only stopped over here for a couple of days on my way to someplace else), I ask whether Brian ever brings any girls home to fuck.

"Up until about a year ago I gather he was still fucking girls," Dave tells me. "But now I think it's strictly boys. He's coming out of the closet with a vengeance."

"What kind of boys?"

"Young athletic types, a couple of years younger than he is. I think he's also into kink. I know he bought himself a black leather jacket recently. And a couple of weeks ago, I found some rope and clothespins in the basement. I *don't* think he was doing laundry."

Shortly after Dave leaves for work the next morning, I explore the bedroom again. In fact I find myself annoyed when, after having left once already, Dave comes back ten minutes later for some work files he forgot. It's the same kind of exasperation one feels trying to get settled down to good sex (or just jacking off) and the phone keeps ringing or a roommate keeps tapping at the door with a gingerly, "I hate to interrupt you, but can I borrow a few dollars?" "I hate to interrupt you *again,* but can I . . ."

Standing in Brian's room, I feel a sensation like vertigo for a moment, as if I'm standing on a high bridge looking down at a river at night: one sees only the glints of reflection off the water, but not the river itself. Like most gay men, I'm fascinated by guys I know about, have heard about, but have never actually met. I don't know why exactly. I remember as a boy I sometimes used to go through my older brother's bedroom when he wasn't home. His room seemed mysterious and exciting to me. I was fascinated by his secrets, the icons of his masculinity, the private souvenirs of his male life; even the smells could fill me with longing, make me ache, as if they belonged to a foreign country I had never visited but was still nostalgic for. I was fascinated by his friends' secrets, too, as if the contents of their jeans pockets or the things they carried around inside their cars had some special significance.

To the left of Brian's closet is an orange crate full of skiing magazines, plus half-a-dozen or so books: *Man's Body: An Owner's Manual, Sex and the Single Guy,* a cheap well-worn paperback entitled *Abnormal Sexual Behavior: 16 Explicit Case Histories of Bizarre Acts,* and others. Whole sections of the *Abnormal Sexual Behavior* book have come unglued from the spine; the book is barely holding together.

Various clothes are scattered around the room: an old green khaki army jacket that smells faintly of old closets, a pair of Adidas socks with filthy soles, hiking boots with dried

26

mud on them, a couple of muscle shirts (one with a button
pinned on it, "I Brake for Hot Buns"), a dirty T-shirt with
the stains of an afternoon's sweat still on it. . . .

The top of his dresser is neat and orderly. He has one of
those tall, narrow oak dressers from the thirties; the edges
of the surface are marred by decades of cigarette burns. Some
pocket change in a glass ashtray, a couple of toothpicks, a
Coca-Cola can from Saudi Arabia. There's also a used disposable razor, with some chips of dark blond hair still on
the blade. The top of the dresser smells soapy, of after-shave,
as if someone had once had an accident with a bottle of
cologne and the wood was now soaked through forever with
that overpowering scent.

On the floor at the foot of the bed, partly hidden by the
ends of the blankets, is another pair of dirty underwear, as
if Brian had slipped them off his hips in the middle of the
night and kicked them way down under the covers — or
maybe he woke up early in the morning and wanted to jack
off.

I pick them up. They're incredibly soft, like the flesh of
a boy's ass. Strange to think of all the erections that must
have occurred in them. What was he thinking about the last
time he had a hard-on in this exact pair of briefs? What was
he imagining himself doing? What — who — was he hunger-
ing for? I imagine his rear — that "creamy, white, flawless"
ass again — tucked into them; and from the front, a trail of
golden dark hair starting around his navel and then trailing
down to disappear beneath the tight waistband. . . .

Other details. There are two posters on the wall: a poster

from some jazz festival in southern California and a ski poster from Switzerland. I hesitate briefly before looking in his dresser drawers. Jockstraps, socks, several brochures from Soloflex. A brochure for one of those "How to Make Your Life's Goals Come True" home-study programs. A generous supply of condoms (Trojan, Regulars). Half a ticket from a Bruce Springsteen concert several years ago. An old beige T-shirt with a fading black message stenciled on the front: "FOR SALE: Almost new chassis with high-speed rear. Must be tested to fully appreciate." Other clothes, the kind with holes and rips in them: the kind of clothes you find in everyone's dresser, favorite clothes that no one can ever bring themselves to throw away.

In one drawer there's a small pile of Polaroids stuck together with a rubber band. The pictures are mostly of young people at indiscernible locations. Teenage friends smiling and making silly faces at the camera. Friends drinking beer, playing cards at a picnic table. A couple of nude shots of some guys at a mountain lake. Good-looking guys, college students. There is, though, one really graphic and sleazy picture (there's no indication of who it is or when it was taken): the snapshot shows a tight, good-looking young ass lowering itself onto an almost impossibly large dildo. In fact, the mammoth dildo is already a good three or four inches into the rectum. On the right cheek of the ass are the words, written with a black-felt pen in big, awkward letters, "Property of J.J.B."

◦ ◦ ◦

28

Later that night — it's probably two or three in the morning —
I wake up hearing voices from the hallway, and the sound
of doors opening and slamming shut. There's a sliver of light
coming from underneath my door and shadows moving back
and forth across it.

"What are you doing back already?" I hear Dave ask, in
a loud whisper.

"A fuckin' drag" . . . "my asshole mother" — a few other
muffled remarks. I can't hear any of it very well. There's
more conversation, the sound of a guy taking a piss and then
washing his hands, and finally a door — Brian's bedroom
door — closing shut. I can hear the thud of him tossing a pair
of shoes in the corner, then opening some drawers, hanging
something in the closet. Silence for a few moments. Then
the click of a light. He must have gone to bed. I wait.
Nothing.

Sometime after that, after I've dozed off for a while, I
suddenly hear the unmistakable sounds of a guy jacking off.
There's the muted creaking of bedsprings, a pause, more
creaking, some low moaning, another pause, more creaking,
and deep breathing. I can tell the exact instant of his eja-
culation: it sounds for a moment like someone bursting up
through the surface of a pool and gasping for air.

Then, silence.

Early the next morning at breakfast, I ask Dave whether
Brian came in last night.

"Yeah. He didn't have a very good time at home. He and

his mother are always getting into it. She's constantly hassling
him." He mimics the voice of a nagging old woman: " 'What
are you doing with your life? When are you going to grow
up? Why don't you at least *try* to get married?' He decided
to come back early."

"Do they know he's gay?"

"He told them last winter. The father took it okay, but
the mother freaked out totally. She started telling everyone,
'I have no son. . . .' "

"So do I get to meet him or what?"

Dave shrugs. "He'll probably sleep till noon. He got in
around three-thirty. And we have to leave pretty soon if you
want to catch your bus. . . ."

Going back up to the guest room, I pause by Brian's
bedroom door, now closed. Strange to think of him in there
now, sleeping, oblivious. I hang around outside his room for
a few minutes, hoping that maybe, just maybe, he'll suddenly
come staggering out — this beautiful boy with the flawless
ass — to take a piss or say hello or get something to eat. . . .

Suddenly I hear the shower go on in the bathroom behind
me. The sound makes me jump. The bathroom door is half-
open. I hesitate for a second, then finally decide to walk in
on the pretext of washing my hands.

Furls of warm steam hit my face. There's a small window
in the wall behind the shower, and I can see a silhouette
against the opaque shower curtain, just the outline of his
head, his shoulders, his arms, and — when he turns slightly —
the seductive line of his ass and an intimation of his cock
and balls. He's lathering up his belly and crotch.

I turn on the water at the sink.

The silhouette suddenly freezes. "Dave?" he calls out, loud enough to be heard over the shower. "Is that you?" The same masculine, reasonably sexy voice I remember from our brief phone conversation.

"Naw," I tell him. "Just me."

Pause.

"How's it goin'?" he asks, starting to soap himself up again nonchalantly.

"Pretty good," I tell him. "And you?"

"Could be better. . . ."

A single hand suddenly shoots out from behind the shower curtain. "Could you hand me that bottle of shampoo on the counter?" I stare at the hand. The underwear, the volleyball, the leather jacket, the porn magazines, the joint, the rubbers — all of them belong to this hand. Staring at it, I find myself wondering, is this the hand he uses to play with his dick? Or is it the other one? I feel that same sharp pang again, just like the one I felt that first day when I saw his dirty jeans lying on the floor in the doorway.

"Sure . . . ," I tell him.

I hand him the bottle — our fingers never touch — and the hand disappears again inside the shower curtain, back to lathering up armpits and his ass and washing his hair.

Then, hearing Dave yell from downstairs that we're going to miss the bus, I reluctantly walk out.

SERENADE FOR FEMALE WITH FANTASIES

Ann Marie Mardith

•

These are the thoughts of an old woman in a dry season, years from sex.

From the heart to the groin, the path grows heavy with cactus, sagebrush, and fireweed. If I bend to pick a cattail, dust clouds my throat and makes me cough. In the thick high grass, cobwebs glisten on shrunken hearts, headless toy soldiers, timid and tattered guts.

Indifferent to used up fancies and muddy romances, sleep comes before I do. My body shrugs at such tired lusts. "Bring me fresh blossoms, mimosa, fuchsia, azaleas, cool green ivy and jasmine rivers if I am to make this great whale arch and plummet, curl up and stretch out like a cat."

My friend Danny won't date. "I go long periods without

sex." I laugh. What to do, I say, with sagging breasts, crusty feet, more here, less there? I worry dark lights will be needed.

Between now, when time quilts a laugh line from my nose to my mouth, and then, when the garment is hemmed and sized and my jowls hang loose in the pockets of my face, I fear nothing will crawl between me and white sheets but clots of dust and lost daddy long legs.

My heart yawns, slouches to the couch and turns on the tube.

My mind, however, in daydreams, on seamless lollygagging days, cavorts in the swamp-soaked gondolas of Venice, the besotted boat skimming dizzily through diamond liquid lanes; somersaults in the meek professor's den on his Hindustan rug; tangos on marble museum floors with decadent Degas; perches salaciously on sweaty steel machines in antiseptic spas; tumbles onto a brass bed in the boss's office; saunters, hands on hips, in the faceless vestibules of bureaucracies, rises and falls in its steel tubes, their sliding doors parting quietly for a shiver of a second and seizing shut as you lean to peek.

On all the floors in the mazes of the highrises where I breathe my hours, in meetings around tables, I find myself in this corner and that, in the corridors of the everyday.

Inveigling with pink lilies and nimble fingers they come courting, slithering from behind on tiger feet, and my mind, not yet pummeled into quietude, ruffles and billows, twitters and squirms. They creep up on my middle age when I'm not looking, nudge a penis into my belly, roll it over until it slides and jiggles, wiggles and thumps, wallops the muscles and chimes bingo.

But my body avoids me.

Just two years ago I was young. I spent hours, imagining Danny, let's say, in bed with me, let's say, his huge bulk in my flowered bedroom like the Merrill Lynch bull, imagining the line of his thigh with the flesh hanging loose and what muscles will contract as he curls his back.

Some women get a bang out of anonymous blue jeans, balls pocketed in tight packaging like garlic bulbs. I, alas, demand the specific man, his skin electrifying the hairs in my ear and the prints of my fingers, this one stolid as a post planted in soil, mind akimbo, one Ichabod Crane with a brackish taste, the next tumbling fat like a giant nude cherub, one gangly, limbs slipping and sliding to the north and south of him.

I knew them cold from the crooked penis to the leg muscles' slack asleep on the sheet, from the too-thin bicep to the ball-shaped calf, from the hair on the arm to the wrist white cold skin. I knew the dead flesh, the smooth chest, the acrid salt on my tongue. I tasted, sniffed, feathered and poked, and wrapped my breathing around them.

But now when my mind sneaks off on a lark — on how this charlatan at fifty sprouts scarcely a paunch, on this one's clear grey eyes in a duplicitous face, how that rake reads my body like a grocery store scanner, on how one or the other might sugar my skin — paper-thin loves mothballed in old blue trunks seep in like smells through clothing in a Chinese restaurant. They remind me that tenderness on demand is not as easy as going to market for a good cut of meat and soaking it overnight in marinade.

Soon, I assume, the twinging in my groin, the tightening of the muscle between my legs, the awkward and defenseless cowering when movies copulate or imply it, will limp into the Alzheimer's of my memory.

And with them those days when sex harasses my skin, trickling into each pore like humid summer air. Taking pictures, for instance, a friend's lover loops around my shoulder. I yell at heart, resist sinking into his chest, cotton shirt to cotton shirt. But my breast, with a life of its own, flips out and jumps him as I pass by.

In a truck squeezed between two men, nerves shoot beyond my fingers, radar scanning for warm objects, pleading with the driver's arm until the strong hand on the gear shift pokes my thigh. At 45, in the township of middle age, I have become a man, copping a feel.

Walking through St. Paul today, I see men in their twenties stripped to their jeans, lording it over the brick and stone houses at Summit and Dale, on ladders and roofs and barely green grass, whistling and shouting, Davids with cigarettes hanging in their mouths, boomboxes singing like teakettles.

I want to suck in every move of the tan muscles on their backs, arms firmed to taut by dumbbells and work. I want my pelvis to flood, swells trespassing from the left of my ass like a snake, over and under my tailbone, crescendoing up my ribs. I want to purr with sweetness and harmony, raunchiness and discord, sensations careening from the heart to the vulva, gyrating and spiraling, but I would have to skulk around the block a hundred times to get my fill.

Still, I'd like to walk this neighborhood dressed in a sheer black lace dress, long sleeves, high neck, cinched at the waist with leather, no slip, a black brassiere, my breasts rising, cleavage agape, spike heels with seamed stockings attached to fine garters, black silk panties.

Instead I camouflage in baggy pants, baggy tops and putty-colored walking shoes, my only concession the lipstick on my mouth and the blush on my cheeks.

Which I wouldn't need if I were to do what I would like to: walk into the garden, you first with your cigarette and leather jacket, then you, then you on the roof, for exhibitionism, you on the ladder, for danger, and you on the grass with your blue eyes and bare chest for rain and the blues.

But sometimes at night, less and less, maybe once a month, maybe every three, I dream with 45-year-old pot-bellied hairy-armed men. He kisses me. I sigh. I kiss him. He sighs. He turns away. I close my eyes. My muscles clench in spite of myself. It reminds me that long ago I was with someone and I spread my heart and my soul and my thighs, and the hair on my arms raised to meet his.

from
VOX
A Novel

Nicholson Baker

•

"Ooh, don't say that or I'll shoot."

"Hah hah! I like a man who knows what he likes. Do you want to hear what I thought about when I came in the shower yesterday?"

"Yes."

"I'll tell you. No, I know what I'll tell you. First I'm going to tell you something else. First I'm going to tell you about how I masturbated in front of somebody. It's short."

"By all means, tell me."

"Shall I tell you every nasty thing that comes into my head?"

"Yes."

"I will then," she said. "We went to the circus. It's funny, it excites me quite a bit just to tell you that I'm going to tell you. Doing that is probably the best part. It's just like that moment when you're lumbering around on the bed to get into opposite directions to do sixty-nine, that feeling of parting my legs over a man's face, *before* you put your hands on my back and pull me down, and my legs remember the feeling from the last time, the feeling of being locked into a preset position that is right for human bodies to be in, like putting a different lens on a camera, turning it until it clicks."

"And I," he said, "would feel the mattress change its slope, first on one side of my head, and then the other, as the weight of one of your knees and then the other pressed into it, and I'd look up at you and open my mouth and I'd slide my hands over your ass with my fingers splayed and hold your ass and pull you down to my tongue."

"Kha."

There was a pause.

"You there?" he asked.

"Yes."

"Tell me about the circus."

"Okay. Excuse me. I'm going to have to get a fresh towel pretty soon. This guy took me to the circus."

"The guy with the fancy stereo?"

"Another guy," she said. "It wasn't Ringling Brothers, it was some smaller-scale South American circus, with lots of elephants, and lots of women in spangles riding the elephants. It was incredibly hot in the tent, and everything had this reddish tint, because the sun was bright enough outside to make it through some of the tent seams, and I was wearing shorts and a T-shirt but I was soaked, and so was Lawrence,

who was also wearing shorts and a T-shirt, and so was everyone around us, including the performers. There was some
Venezuelan act in which a woman spun hard balls around
very fast on long strings while two men played percussion
behind her, and the balls smacked against the floorboards in
interesting rhythms around her legs, and she was *streaming*
with sweat, and quite beautiful, but in a way that I thought
was vaguely like me, and suddenly the two men would stop
hitting the drums and she would freeze and make this kind
of trilling scream, a beautiful strange wild sound. She was
just covered with sweat, she looked really wild, and the two
men behind her were exceedingly good-looking, wearing
wide-brimmed hats with chin straps, and I momentarily
wanted to be her, and while they were taking their bows I
adapted my time-tested striptease fantasy, and I thought that
I was this woman in the black spangles, and I was spinning
these balls very fast, faster than she could, so they were a
blur, so fast that somehow, like in a cartoon fight when it's
just a blur from which things, pieces of clothing, fly outward,
somehow my whole outfit was torn in pieces from my body,
and flung out into the audience, so that when the drumming
stopped and I froze suddenly and made my trilling scream,
I was totally naked, and all these pieces of my costume were
still floating aloft in all directions, and each man who caught
some damp shred of costume was overpowered and took his
place in line to fuck me, and the two percussionists played
the drums the whole time, and then they stopped drumming
and naturally they fucked me too. But that's just an aside.
The elephant acts were what were interesting. I've ridden

on an elephant once or twice in my life, when I was small, and I remember touching the big lobes of its head, and let me tell you, the skin is not smooth, it's warm and dry and quite bristly — that's how I remember it, anyway. And these were not little elephants, these were big old elephants, with big tusks. Well, these women were sliding down the side of the elephants, riding on the elephants' heads, with their legs between the elephants' eyes, and repeatedly pivoting around on their bottoms on the elephants' backs, and they were wearing flesh-colored stockings, or tights, so it was not skin to skin, but even so, those little leotards are cut extremely high in the back, and I really started to be concerned about their bottoms, about whether they were more uncomfortable than their smiles let on, and I started thinking about whether if *I* were dressed in a very high-cut leotard I would like the sensation of the elephant's dry living skin on my bottom, and then, during the beginning of the very last big elephant promenade, one of the women was riding on the elephant's back with one leg in the air, and as the elephant turned I saw this woman's bottom, and even through the tights I could see that it was in fact red! She was the main elephant woman, I think. Anyhow, for the big finale she rode around on this elephant's tusks for a minute or two, sat on his trunk, fine fine, all gracefully executed but surprisingly suggestive, and then she did this thing that really shocked me. She took hold of one of the tusks and one of the ears, or somehow swung herself up, and then she lifted one of her knees so that it went right *into* the elephant's mouth, and she waited for a second for the elephant to clamp on to it, and then she threw her head back, and arched her back, and spread her arms wide, so she was held in the air supported entirely by her knee, which was stuffed in the elephant's mouth! I mean, think about the saliva! Think about those elephant molars that are gently but firmly taking hold of your upper calf and your mid-thigh, while this elephant tongue is there lounging with its giant taste-buds against your knee! The elephant did a full turn while she was swooning like this. Then she got down and took a bow and patted the elephant under his eye."

"Wow, that's better than *King Kong*."

"Well *I* was impressed. Lawrence had come up with the idea of going to the circus — this was our very first time out, by the way, though I'd known him for a while — so he was careful not to be too impressed. While we were walking out to the car he said, 'I guess those elephants really respond to training.' He thought the elephant wasn't biting the woman's leg, but rather that its tongue was actually hooked under her knee. I was dubious, but it was an interesting idea. It was touching to see how pleased Lawrence was that I'd liked the circus. We were standing out by my car in the parking lot, just drenched with sweat, he was plucking at his shirt and squinting at me, and we were supposed to go to this clam-shack place and have an early dinner on a picnic table outside, and I just didn't want to do that. So I thought what the hell, and I said, 'You look hot. Why don't you come back to my apartment and you'll have a shower, and I'll have a shower and then I'll make some dinner and we'll do the clam shack another time, okay?' He agreed instantly — he was delighted to have the responsibility for the success of this date taken out of his hands. So he had a shower, and I happened to have a pair of very baggy shorts with an elastic waistband that fit him fine, and a big T-shirt, and then I had a shower, and I put on a pair of shorts and a dark red T-shirt, and everything was fine."

"But separate showers, no nudity."

"No, very chaste," she said.

"What was he doing when you got out of the shower?"

"He was peering inside a Venetian paperweight."

"Classic. He'd obviously heard your shower turn off, and then he'd stood there, holding the paperweight to his face for ten minutes, so that you would be sure to discover him in that casual pose, appreciating your trinket."

"Quite possible. Anyhow, he sat in the kitchen and we talked rather formally while I made a spiral kind of pasta and microwaved a packet of creamed chipped beef — this is a great dish, incidentally, Stouffer's creamed chipped beef over any kind of pasta noodles — I have it about once a week. Lawrence made an elaborate pretense of being impressed by this super easy recipe, and when I poured the spirals from the drainer into a bowl he came over to where I was standing and said, 'I have to see this.' I was going to simply slice the packet of creamed chipped open and dump it over the spirals, which is what I normally do, but I was feeling sneaky, I'd just had a shower, and you know about me and showers, but I hadn't dithered, despite the *major* striptease fantasy I'd had at the circus, because obviously I couldn't, since a man was in my apartment, so I was feeling devious, and so I got out some olive oil and poured a little of it on the spirals, and he — he was definitely not in the know about cooking, and I'm certainly not much of a cook myself — but he said, 'So *that's* how you keep them from sticking and clumping.' I stirred them up, and they made an embarrassingly luscious sexy sound, and I just decided, fuck it, I've dressed this person, I'm feeding this person, I'm going to seduce this person, right now, today, so I said, I said, 'How very strange,' I said, 'I just remembered something I haven't thought of in years. I just remembered this kid in my junior high — you remind me of him in some ways — I just remembered his commenting that a certain girl must have used olive oil to put on her jeans.' Well, I saw Lawrence's little eyeballs roll at this. He said something obvious about extra virgin cold pressed and he snuffed out a nervous laugh and I thought, yes, I am in charge here, I am going to see this person's penis get hard, and even though I have a smoldering yeast problem and so can't really have full-fledged sex I am going to have my way with this person somehow. It was probably that Venezuelan ball-twirling screamer that put me in that mood, now that I think back. I mean, I felt powerful and shrewd and effortlessly in control and everything else I usually don't feel. I cut open the packet of creamed chipped and I said, musingly, 'My grandmother was very careful about money — she always used to say that she was as tight as the bark on a tree. And I used to think about what that really would feel like, whether bark does feel tight to the inner wood of the tree. I used to put on my jeans and take them off, thinking about that.' Lawrence said, 'Really!' I said, 'Yeah, although actually I didn't like my jeans to be at all tight, even then. I liked them loose. The appeal was the rough fabric, and the rough stitching, very barklike, the appeal was of being in this sort of complete male embrace, but then when you took them off, being all smooth and curved.' Lawrence nodded seriously. So I said, making the leap, I said, 'And when I started getting my legs waxed, which is quite an expensive little procedure, I also thought of that phrase, *as tight as the bark on a tree*, when Leona, my waxer, began putting the little warm wax strips on my legs and letting them solidify for an instant and ripping them off.' I said, 'In fact, I just had my legs waxed yesterday.' Lawrence said, 'Is that right?' and I said, 'Yes, it's amazing how much freer you feel after your legs are waxed — it's almost as if you've become physically more limber — you want to leap around, and make high kicks, cavort.' I waited for that to sink in and then I said, 'Leona's a tiny Ukrainian woman, and she makes this growly sound as she rips the strips of muslin and wax off, *rrr*, and when she's done both my legs and there's no more hurting, she rubs lotion into them, and it's a surprisingly sensual experience.' Lawrence was silent for a second and then he said, 'I'm inexperienced with depilatory techniques. I've never known anyone who had her legs waxed.' I said, 'Let's have dinner.' "

"What a tactician!"

"Not really. Anyhow, we had dinner, which was pretty tame. Lawrence had many virtues, he had a kind of bony broad-shoulderedness, and a deliberate way of blinking and looking at you when you spoke, and he was quite smart — he was a patent lawyer."

"Ah. Patent in*fringe*ment?"

"Yes indeed. But he had no conversational skills at all. He was putty in my hands. No, I'm actually making myself seem more completely sure of my powers than I felt — but still, I was pretty much in control. I started asking him how electrical things worked — you know, like what shortwave radio was, and how cordless telephones worked, and why it is that at drive-ins now you can hear the movie on the FM radio in your car. And he was full of interesting information, once you jump-started him that way. But the thing was, I kept a faint racy undertone going in the conversation. For instance, I'd say, 'What do you think those ham-radio buffs really talked about? Do you think some of them were secretly gay, and they left their wives asleep and crept down to their finished basements in the middle of the night to have long conversations with *friends* in New Zealand or wherever?' He said, 'I suppose it's a possibililty.' And about the drive-ins I said things like, 'It must be much more comfortable and *private* in drive-ins now, because you can close the window completely, you don't have that metal thing hanging there with the tinny sound, covered with yellow chipped paint, like a chaperone, you're not attached to anything around you, it's much more like being in a car on the expressway.' He said he didn't know exactly how drive-ins supplied FM sound, because he hadn't been to a drive-in since he was eight years old, but he said that technically speaking it was an easy problem to solve, for instance there was a thing advertised in the back of *Popular Science* that picks up any sound in the room and broadcasts it to FM radios within several hundred yards, and it's called a Bionic Mike Transmitter. I said, 'Ooo, a Bionic Mike Transmitter!' He said, 'Oh sure, it's this device that you can leave in this room, for instance, and it will broadcast any sound in the room to any nearby FM radio, if it's correctly tuned.' He said, 'Of course it's advertised with a big warning about how it's not meant for illegal surveillance. But probably that's what it's used for.' I said, 'You mean that whatever I did, whatever intimate private activity I engaged in, would be heard by the people swooshing by in the cars on the expressway?' He said, 'If they were tuned correctly, yes.' I said, 'Hmmm.' You see, my living room is on the second floor, about three hundred feet from a raised part of the expressway.''

"In some eastern city," he said.

"That's right," she said.

"So what did Lawrence do when you expressed a keen interest in his description of the Bionic Mike Transducer?"

"Transmitter. He asked if he could have a fourth helping of creamed chipped beef. Then we were finished and I started to clear the table and he said, 'I'll wash up.' I said, 'No, forget it, I'll do it later,' but he said, 'No no really, I like washing up.' So I said fine, and he cleaned the kitchen, quite efficiently, while I told him the plot of *Dial M for Murder*, really lingering over the hot letter that's found on the body of the man with the pair of scissors in his back. You know? Lawrence listened carefully—he'd never seen the movie, if you can believe it. He said he didn't like black-and-white movies. I said, 'Fine, don't like them, *Dial M for Murder* is in color.' He said, 'Oh.' And then he said, 'Well, I think Hitchcock was a fairly sick individual anyway.' I said, 'You're probably right.' Then he dried his hands with a paper towel and turned toward me holding the glass bottle of olive oil and he said, 'Now, where does this go?' I said, 'Well, where would you like it to go?' And he said, 'I don't know.' So I said, 'Well sometimes, after I get my legs waxed, the day after, they're still a little tender, and I've found that olive oil really helps them feel better.' Which wasn't true, they feel fine the day after, but anyway."

"Erotic license."

"Exactly. He said, 'But that would be terriby messy!' I said, 'So I'll stand in the bathtub.' And he said, 'But won't it be cold and clammy?' So I turned the bottle of oil on its side and put it in the microwave for twenty seconds. He felt it and he shook his head and said, 'I think it needs a full minute.' So we leaned on the counter, looking at the micro- wave, while it heated the oil. When the five beeps beeped, Lawrence took it out, and we went to the bathroom together. I stood in the bathtub and pulled my shorts up high on my legs, and very solemnly he poured a little pool of olive oil on his fingers and rubbed it just above my knee."

"He was kneeling himself?"

"Yes. The bathtub wasn't really wet anymore — I mean it was still humid from both the showers, but we didn't have the water running or anything. He said, 'You're very smooth.' I said, 'Thank you.' A rather powerful smell of olive oil surrounded us, and I began to feel quite Mediterranean and Bacchic, and honestly somewhat like a mushroom being lightly sautéed. He stared at his hand going over my skin, blinking at it. I pulled the sides of my shorts up higher so he could do more of my thighs, and I said, 'Leona is very thorough. No follicle is left unmolested.' Then, whoops, I wondered whether that was maybe too kinky for him and whether he might think that I was trying to give him the idea that Leona had gone over the edge and waxed off all my pubic hair, horrifying thought, so I said, 'I mean, within limits.' He just kept on dolloping oil on his fingers and rubbing it in. After a while I turned around and held on to the showerhead and he did the backs of my legs. He wasn't artful at all, he didn't know how to knead the deep muscles, but I could feel the intelligence and interest in his fingers when they came to each new dry curve. His hands went right up underneath the bagginess of my shorts. I liked that. He didn't say anything. Once I think he cleared his throat. Finally he said, 'Okay, I think that's everything.' I turned around and looked down at him: he was sitting with his legs crossed, looking at my legs, very closely, really letting his eyes travel over them. He had curly hair — he needed a haircut, in fact. He had the top of the olive oil in one hand and the bottle in the other, and before he stood up he pressed the circle of the plastic top back and forth up the inside of both my legs, in a zigzag. Then he stood up and handed me the bottle. He was blushing. I smiled at him and I said, 'Are you suffering from any sticking or clumping?' And he said, 'Yeah, some.' So I pulled on the waistband of his shorts and poured about a tablespoonful of oil in there."

"No kidding!"

"Yes, well, he looked at me with shock. And I know I

wouldn't have been able to do it if they hadn't really been my *own* shorts that I'd lent him. I said, 'I'm awfully sorry, I don't know what I was thinking. Take those off and I'll see if I have another pair.' So he marched that peculiar march that men do as they are taking off their pants. He was not erect by any means, but he wasn't dormant either. I said, 'Did the olive oil feel warm?' And he said, 'Yes.' So I said, 'Would you like some more?' and he said, 'Maybe.' So I held the mouth of the bottle right where his pubic hair bushed out, high on his cock, I mean near the base, not near the tip, because he was still drooping down, and I tipped it as if to pour it over him, but I didn't actually let any come out. I just held it three. And the expectation of the warmth of the oil made his cock rise a little. I tipped the bottle even more, so that the olive oil was right in the neck, ready to pour out, but still I didn't actually pour it. And his erection rose a little more, wanting the oil. It was like some kind of stage levitation. His hands were in little boyish fists at his sides. When he was almost horizontal, but still angling slightly downward, suddenly I poured the entire rest of the bottle over him, just *glug glug glug glug glug,* so that it flowed down its full cock length and fell with a buzzing sound onto the bathtub. And this was not a trivial amount of oil, this was about maybe a third of the bottle. The waste was itself exciting. It was like covering him in some amber glaze. He hurriedly moved his legs farther apart so he wouldn't get oil spatter on his feet. By the time there were only a few last drips falling from the bottle, he was totally, I mean totally, hard. And of course with this success I had second thoughts. I almost wanted him to leave right then so that I could come in the shower by myself. I stepped out of the tub and I said, 'Sorry, I got carried away. And the problem is, I have this darn yeast situation, so I can't really do anything with that magnificent thing, much as I'd like to.' He said, 'Ah, that's all right, I'll just go home and take care of that myself, that's no problem,' he said, 'but your *tub*, on the other hand, is a mess. Ask me to clean it and I will.' I said, 'Oh don't worry about that, it's just oil, it's nothing.' But he was on his own private trajectory, and he said, 'That's right, it's oil, plus I have to say the tub is not terribly clean to begin with.' I said, 'No no no, don't even think of it, really.' He picked up an old dry Rescue pad that was in a corner and he held it up and said, 'Look, tell me to clean your tub.' He's standing there, a pantless patent lawyer, semi-erect, wearing my Danger Mouse T-shirt, holding the tiny curled-up green Rescue pad with a fierce expression. *He wanted to clean my tub.* I said, 'Well, great. Please do. Sure.' He asked for some Ajax, so I brought some from the kitchen, along with a folding chair so I could sit and watch. Well, this Lawrence turned out to be some kind of demon scrub-wizard. He hands me my bottles of shampoo, one by one. My tub is now naked! He squats in it, so that his testicles are practically gamboling in the giant teardrop of oil that's on the bottom, and he takes the Ajax and he taps its rim against the edge of the tub, all the way around, so that these *curtains* of pale blue powder fall down the sides, kind of an aurora borealis effect, and then he moistens his Rescue pad and he starts scrubbing and scrubbing, every curve, every seam, talk about circling motions, my lord! He did the place where the shampoo bottles had been, that I'd simply defined as a safe haven for mildew, he was in there, *grrr, grrrr,* twisting and jamming that little sponge. Not that my tub is filthy, it isn't, it's just not sparkling, and there *is* a faint rich smell of mildew or something vaguely biological, which I kind of like, because it's so closely associated by now with my private shower activity. But here I was watching this guy *in* my shower! He took down the Water Pik massage head and he rinsed off the parts he'd done, and he began to herd all the oil down the drain with hot water, and the oil and the Ajax had mixed and formed this awful stuff, like a *roux* first, and then when the water mixed in it became this yellow sort of foam, which didn't daunt him, he took care of it. And then he started scrubbing his way toward the fittings, using liberal amounts of Ajax alternating with hot water. He said, 'You don't worry about scratching, do you?' I said I didn't. So he gnarled around the cold-water tap and he gnarled around the hot-water tap and he circled fiercely around the clitty thing that controls the drain, and then when the whole rest of the tub was absolutely *gleaming,* he went to the drain itself — he set aside the filter thing, and he reached two fingers way in, and he pulled out this revolting slime locket and splapped it against the side of the tub, and then he really went to work on that drain, around and around the rim of chrome, and deeper, right down to those dark crossbars, that I'd never gotten to, he worked the scrubber sponge in there, *grrr,* more Ajax, more circling, more hot water. I mean I was in a transport!"

"I bet."

"Then I held out the trash can, and he threw out the drain slime and the Rescue pad, and he rinsed his hands, and he stood, and in the midst of this newly cleaned tub he started to rinse off his cock and his legs, where a little oil had fallen, and I watched the water go over him, I watched the way the even spray of the showerhead in his hand made all the hairs on his legs into these perfect perfect rows, like some ideal crop, and he was quite hairy, and so I slipped off my shorts and unders and sat on the far end of the bathtub and propped my left foot against a washcloth handle and I hung my right leg out over the edge of the bathtub, so I was wide open, and I said, 'I'm a bit rank, too, do me,' so he started playing the water over my legs and then directly on my . . . femalia, and I held my lips open so that he could see my inner wishbone, and the drops of water exploding on it, and as he sprayed me, he began to get hard again. But I can't come with just water, so I started strumming myself, while he sprayed my hand, which was a lovely feeling, and I held out my left hand and he maneuvered closer to me and I took hold of his cock and tried to begin to jerk it off, but I didn't do very well, because my own finger on my clit felt so good, and I couldn't seem to keep the two kinds of mas-turbating motion going with my left and right hand inde-pendently, I was making big odd circles with his cock, so instead I took the showerhead from him and I said, 'You're on your own,' and I sprayed his cock and some of his Danger Mouse T-shirt, that is, *my* Danger Mouse T-shirt, while he began stroking away, staring at my legs and my pussy, and I liked spraying him quite a lot, I liked aiming the water at

his fist, I liked the sight of his wet T-shirt, and he had, this
is rather bad of me to say, but he had a kind of gruesome-
looking cock, a real monster, and the relief of not having
that girth in me was itself almost enough to put me over the
top, and it looked quite a bit more distinguished through the
glint of the spray. But I also wanted the water on me — I
wanted to spray him, but I wanted the water flowing on me
as well — and suddenly it seemed like the most natural thing
in the world, I remembered the elephant woman lifting her
knee, and so I reached forward and pulled his hips toward
me so that his legs straddled my left leg, and I lifted my
knee, and he clamped his thighs around it, and I let my other
leg sprawl so that I was absolutely wide open, and now,
when I sprayed his cock and his hand the water streamed
down his thighs and then down my thigh and on me. And
it was exactly what I wanted, and it started to feel so good,
and I said so, and suddenly he started stroking himself incredibly fast, it was this blur, like a *sewing* machine, and he
produced this major jet of sperm at a diagonal right into the
circular spray of the water, so that it fought against all the
drops and was sort of torn apart by them, and he was clamping my leg, my smooth leg, extremely tight with those perfectly water-groomed thighs, and I shifted adroitly so that
the poached sperm and hot-water runoff wouldn't pour directly into me and possibly cause trouble, but so that it still
poured over me. And then he took the showerhead again,
and still holding his cock and still clamping my knee very
tight, he sprayed slowly across my hand and my thighs very
close with the water until I closed my eyes and came, imag-

ining I was in front of a circus audience. So that was nice."

"God of mercy, I am so jealous!"

"Don't be," she said. "I think my offhand talk of yeast unnerved him, and his subservient streak unnerved *me*. Anyway, the point is, that story is connected to this very call between you and me, because when I was in the shower yesterday, and close to coming —"

"Thinking about the three painters."

"No, *after* the three painters, when I was very close to coming, I was thinking of that time with Lawrence, as I occasionally do, I imagine him handing me my bottles of shampoo with a serious expression, or some fragment of it, anyway yesterday I thought of the Bionic Mike Transmitter that he'd described, and I started to make these very theatrical moans, like 'oh yeah, oh yeah baby, ooh yeah, pump it deep, pump it deep, oooh yeah' and I imagined that someone had left a Bionic Mike Transmitter in my bathroom and that random men on the expressway were driving by with their radios scanning the stations and suddenly they would pick me up, they'd hear me moaning exaggeratedly in the shower. I started to feel myself beginning to come, and I filled my mouth with water, and I thought of the men on the expressway hearing my mouth fill with water, and as I started to come I pushed the water from my mouth so that it poured from my chin over me, which is what I usually do, and I said, and this was not theatrical, this was heartfelt, I said, *'Oh, shoot it, shoot it, you cocksuckers!'* "

WHY:

Bob Flanagan

·

Why: Because it feels good; because it gives me an erection; because it makes me come; because I'm sick; because there was so much sickness; because I say FUCK THE SICK-NESS; because I like the attention; because I was alone a lot; because I was different; because kids beat me up on the way to school; because I was humiliated by nuns; because of Christ and the crucifixion; because of Porky Pig in bondage, force-fed by some sinister creep in a black cape; because of stories about children hung by their wrists, burned on the stove, scalded in tubs; because of "Mutiny on the Bounty"; because of cowboys and indians; because of Houdini; because of my cousin Cliff; because of the forts we built and the things we did inside them; because of what s inside me; because of my genes; because of my parents; because of doctors and nurses; because they tied me to the crib so I wouldn't hurt myself; because I had time to think; because I had time to hold my penis; because I had awful stomach aches and holding my penis made it feel better; because I felt like I was going to die; because it makes me feel invincible; because it makes me feel triumphant; because. I'm a Catholic; because I still love lent, and I still love my penis, and in spite of it all I have no guilt; because my parents said BE WHAT YOU WANT TO BE, and this is what I want to be; because I'm nothing but a big baby and I want to stay that way, and I want a mommy forever, even a mean one, especially a mean one; because of all the fairy tale witches and, and the wicked stepmother, and the stepsisters, and how sexy Cinderella was, smudged with soot, doomed to a life of servitude; because of Hansel, locked in the witch's cage until he was fat enough to eat; because of "O" and how desperately I wanted to be her; because of my dreams; because of the games we played; because I've got an active imagination; because my mother bought me tinker toys; because hardware stores give me hard-ons; because of hammers, nails, clothespins, wood, padlocks, pullies, eyebolts, thumbtacks, staple-guns, sewing needles, wooden spoons, fishing tackle, chains, metal rulers, rubber tubing, spatulas, rope, twine, C-clamps, S-hooks, razor blades, scissors, tweezers, knives, push pins, two-by-fours, ping-pong paddles, alligator clips, duct tape, broom sticks, bar-b-cue skewers, bungie cords, saw horses, soldering irons; because of tool sheds; because of garages; because of basements; because of dungeons; because of *The Pit and the Pendulum*; because of the Tower of London; because of the Inquisition; because of the rack; because of the cross; because of the Addams Family playroom; because of Morticia Addams and her black dress with its octopus legs; because of motherhood; because of Amazons; because of the Goddess; because of the moon; because it's in my nature; because it's against nature; because it's nasty; because it's fun; because it flies in the face of all that's normal (whatever that is); because I'm not normal; because I used to think that I was part of some vast experiment and that there was this implant in my penis that made me do these things and allowed THEM (whoever THEY were) to monitor my activities; because I had to take my clothes off and lie inside this giant plastic bag so the doctors could collect my sweat; because once upon a time I had such a high fever my parents had to strip me naked and wrap me in wet sheets to stop the convulsions; because my parents loved me even more when I was suffering; because I was born into a world of suffering; because surrender is sweet; because I'm attracted to it; because I'm addicted to it; because endorphins in the brain are like a natural kind of heroin; because I learned to take my medicine; because I was a big boy for taking it; because I can take it like a man; because, as somebody once said, HE'S GOT MORE BALLS THAN I DO; because it is an act of courage; because it does take guts; because I'm proud of it; because I can't climb mountains; because I'm terrible at sports; because NO PAIN, NO GAIN; because SPARE THE ROD AND SPOIL THE CHILD; BECAUSE YOU ALWAYS HURT THE ONE YOU LOVE.

MILK

Michael Dorsey

•

Moscow is beautiful in the spring. All cities are beautiful in the spring, but Moscow is more beautiful because after the Russian winter Muscovites need it to be. And when overcoats and boots start to come off the women of the world, and ankles and knees and even thighs come in view of the desperate men of the world, Moscow's women are the most beautiful in the world because they have to emerge from under more layers of shapeless clothing than the women of other great cities, and the miracle of being able to walk down the street and see a thousand different shapes and sizes of breasts press against a thousand different blouses and sweaters, that miracle has been longed for so ardently through the dark and bitter months gone by.

This year the women of Moscow are more beautiful than

ever. They have to be. The winter has never been harder. So many people are out of work. The homeless are everywhere. Food is scarce. The women are unbearably beautiful. Desire hangs shimmering in the air. This can only mean that there will be a great many more mouths to feed next winter, but now it is spring, and the people want to shake off the grim months behind and live again.

Still, the lines are long, and they are everywhere. Lines for bread, lines for sausage, for shoes, for milk.

Milk. When there was nothing else through the long dark years to keep the country alive, there had at least been milk. Milk and vodka. Some prefer the vodka, but others cannot think of their home, of their nation, of life, without thinking of milk.

There is a young man now, going from line to line around the city. There are no lines at the milk stores today because there is no milk. The supplies were gone by noon, and it is now nearly three. But there are lines in front of certain garages and apartment blocks, where the black-market dealers operate, and any one of them could be selling milk.

He hurries from line to line, staying just long enough to find out what is being sold, then hurries on to the next line. He isn't joking or talking politics or showing off to the women, who are ethereally beautiful right now. Everyone has begun to notice it, even the old men are aware of a musky imminence floating on the late-day sun.

The young man is tall and well-built, good enough looking that the women notice him, smile at him. He is as pale as milk himself. He grew up in the Ukraine, but was chosen to become an engineer and brought to Moscow. He knows no one in the city, and isn't likely to. Shyness has led to loneliness and an overwhelming thirst that seeks to fill the empty place. Not a thirst for vodka. He longs for milk. It is the only thing that takes him back to where he wants to be, to the Ukraine, and to his childhood, and away from a city he doesn't like or understand.

The government gave him an apartment and a tiny stipend, and in theory he is still supposed to be waiting for a call that will never come, telling him where to go and what to do to be an engineer. He has no reason to stay, but no reason to go — things are not any better where his parents are. So he stays, and aches, and tries to drown the ache in milk. All the money he has, or can get, everything that he can sell or trade, has gone for milk. Like any other drunk, he cares about nothing but getting another glass, another bottle, and he stumbles around the city in a daze, thinking of nothing but pure, sweet milk.

Today he has chased the black market dealers through every district and found nothing. It's almost dark, and the lines are breaking up. People are going home. Some have succeeded in finding what they wanted. Others have found each other. It's been the first really warm day of the spring, and everyone seems pleased and hopeful, even those who go home with empty arms. The young man turns toward his apartment building, out of habit, and plods along, numb with failure and desire.

A very pretty young woman approaches him. Her face is almost hidden behind heavy makeup, but she is young and can still shine through her own inept artwork. She has on a tight red sweater and even tighter blue jeans. The day is cooling off quickly, but she has left the sweater unbuttoned so that all can see how the sweater presses her breasts together and lifts them up, asking to be touched and kissed. The valley between them is pink with the cool breeze, and her nipples have hardened against the cloth of the sweater. She smiles up at him.

"Would you like to see my apartment? It's very pretty. I live alone."

"No, no. I have to meet someone."

Before he can race away, she catches his hand and presses it against her breast.

"It wouldn't cost much. Not for you."

"I have to get some milk."

She is as surprised by this as he is himself, and she draws her hand away. He stands for a moment looking at her but, unable to think how to explain himself, turns and flees. The one time he looks back she has already approached another man. They are both laughing, but surely, he thinks, about something else. The other fellow's hand is already inside her blouse, warming one of her poor, chilly breasts.

He makes no haste, but soon reaches the square, plain block of flats where he lives. He pauses for a moment just outside, with a dim sense that somehow something will happen to prevent him having to go in unsatisfied. Nothing happens except that the breeze whips up, cooler than before, and he goes in.

Most floors of the building have as many as six separate

apartments, but on his floor there are only two. His own is quite small, and he knows from this just how large the other is. There are as many doors on his floor as on the others, and he assumes that once there were as many flats. He knows nothing about the couple living there. He has seen the man many times, rushing in and out, always well-dressed, graying, purposeful. They nod but they don't talk, and both of them like it that way. He has only seen the woman a few times, through the open door of the apartment, once in the street outside, from the back, walking away.

Maybe the man is a member of the government. He must have some sort of influence, an influence that has grown, and as his power has grown the apartment has slowly swallowed up its neighbors, the walls separating them inside one by one coming down, the doors onto the hallway no longer used. One day soon, the young man thinks, these people will want his apartment too, and will demand it, and it will be given to them — unless the man has lost his prestige with the change of government.

The young man is in the hallway outside their door, when his legs suddenly become useless with lack of purpose and refuse for a moment to continue. He leans against the door of the other couple's flat, the one door they still use. He isn't listening, isn't doing anything at all, and yet he can't help hearing from behind the door the soft crying of a baby. It isn't a plaintive crying, but the self-soothing crying of a baby putting itself to sleep, and still more softly and distantly he hears the cooing of its mother encouraging its efforts, soothing and gentling her baby off to sleep. He has heard a baby

in the building before, but the flats are old, the walls are
thick and he never knew that it was so nearby, that right
across the hall from him a mother and a child were going
through all the rhythmic rituals that are such a distant memory for him. His cheek is pressed against the wood of the
door, and his hand caresses its grain. Without a sound he
too begins to cry, not painfully or loudly, but with all his
soul.

Without thinking, he knocks on the door. He is startled
by the sound and wonders where it comes from. Before he
understands that it was he who made it, the door opens.
There stands the woman. He has never been so close to her
before. She is small, with wide hips and big breasts, swollen
now with milk for her child. She is wearing a sweatshirt with
the name of an American rock and roll band, and blue jeans
that show the shape of her legs and thighs. She is over thirty,
much older than the young man, but her face is soft. She
looks just a little surprised. His face is wet, but he forgets
that. He is a little confused, but the woman doesn't seem
unkind.

"I . . . I heard the baby."

"I'm sorry. He's asleep how."

He wants to say more, but doesn't know what.

"Do you have any milk? I couldn't find any. I looked
everywhere."

"I may have some powdered."

Again, the moment of confusion.

"No, never mind. Thank you."

His legs still won't move, and he stands looking at her,

the tears standing in his eyes. She takes his shoulder and brings him into the flat. As soon as she touches him he is able to move again. She quietly shuts the door, and with no sound and in a single gesture she lifts the sweatshirt over her head. Her breasts are white as milk, as soft as milk, heavy with milk. Her nipples are big and thick and dark. As soon as the shirt is off they begin to wrinkle and reach toward him. She lifts her right breast with her hand and looks at him. He is again paralyzed. As though the breast had been rejected, she lifts the left one and looks at him. Then she understands that he cannot move without her, and she puts her hand behind his neck, to draw him toward her.

She has to reach up, he is so much taller, and as she pulls him toward her she also pulls him down, until he is on his knees before her. His mouth is then just level with the purple nipple he is offered, and he closes his eyes and opens his mouth. She pushes her breast against his lips, and he begins to drink. Her milk is sweet and rich, much better than any he can remember. He throws his arms around her now, his strength returning, and pulls her against him. He sucks too hard, and she gasps and pulls his hair to make him be gentle. He stops for a moment and looks up, not drinking but with his tongue still pressed like a question mark against the tip of her breast. She smiles and pats his hair. Again he closes his eyes, and resumes more gently.

There is so much milk, it seems at first that it will go on forever, but at last it stops. Still he keeps on, gently biting and teasing her nipple, licking her breast all over, whimpering softly, pressing his face against the softness of her.

His hand comes up to her right breast and kneads it, squeezing until a jet of milk spills out across his wrist. He looks at his wrist and licks it, looks at her breast, and starts to lick his way across to it, but she stops him.

"No, it's too late. My husband could come home any time."

He looks up at her from his knees, the confusion again settling over him. He looks around, as if to see where he is, and then he hugs her waist, pressing his cheek against the dampness of her breast, wetting again the tears that have dried there. She pats and gently pulls his hair with both hands, hugs him to her, then pushes him away.

"Come again in the morning. He will be gone all day."

He is again in the hall, not quite sure how, but his legs are once more moving and they take him into his own apartment and his own bed, where he lies all night, not sleeping but nonetheless dreaming. Maybe it isn't even a dream, it is so simple. He dreams of milk, and of the breasts and face of the woman who gave it to him, and he dreams of having more.

In the morning he is alive and awake, well rested as if he had slept. His mind is clear, and all he wants is for the first few hours of daylight to pass so that he can return to the woman. He hears the man leave, but makes himself wait another half hour to be sure he won't return, and then he walks boldly across the hall and knocks. She opens the door at once. Today she is dressed in a leather skirt and nylons, a silk blouse that he can not quite see through. He can see her nipples, already standing up hard against the fabric, rubbing against it every time she moves, making them impatient and irritable with a need like a persistent itch. When she opens the door she makes a small, pleased sound, and he sees a small dark spot where a drop of milk has escaped onto the silk.

In the time when he wasn't dreaming his single dream during the night, he wondered about this moment. Would she want him to kiss her? Did she want to talk? Could anything ever be as simple and clear as the day before? He has no experience in these things and doesn't know what she might expect. As soon as he sees her the doubts begin again, but before they can overwhelm him she has again drawn him inside and shut the door.

Once more without a word she reaches for her blouse. At first her hand grazes the button, but then she hesitates a moment. With the silk still covering them, her hands begin to caress her breasts, rubbing the silk against them and irritating them still more. He watches for a few seconds. Then his own hands reach out and brush hers gently aside, taking their place and moving around and around in circles, lifting the heavy flesh and letting it fall, feeling its weight and bounce, squeezing the hard tip and feeling it get harder still. There are spots on the silk over both breasts now, and both the man and woman have begun to breathe hard, to make small sounds, to sigh and catch their breath. She reaches again for the button, and he pushes her hand away again, more firmly this time, and himself unbuttons her blouse.

As the silk falls away he sees her breasts once again, as full and beautiful as they have been in his mind all night.

He had almost feared that his mind had exaggerated, but nothing could move him more than the way they hang, soft and heavy and fat with her womanhood. He had drunk the day before until her left breast was half the size of its friend, limp and empty, but here it is again as proud and full as it had been, and as he looks at it he too begins to swell.

His patience gone, he falls to his knees again before her and buries his face against her until the milk begins to spurt from her too-full breasts. And then he licks it up from where it falls, on her belly and ribs, making his way back up until he once more reaches the nipple and drinks. This time he knows just how hard he can suck without hurting, and he begins to tease. He pulls a little harder and little harder until he hears her start to gasp and feels her grip on his hair tighten, then he becomes gentle and she sighs. If he becomes too gentle she beats her fists softly on the back of his head and finally presses him against her until he responds by sucking harder.

It doesn't take long, though, until the breast is empty again, and he begins again to bite the nipple and squeeze the breast with his hands to punish it for bringing his supply of milk to an end. He hasn't eaten anything since he first saw her the night before, except the milk that she gave him, and he has a hunger now like never before. He continues to bite and lick her stomach, holding her tightly as he had done the night before.

"The other one. It needs you too."

It is only the third time he has heard her speak, and he has not spoken yet. His voice sounds rusty as he replies:

"You need something for the baby."

"My husband is black market. I do nothing but eat. There's plenty for the baby. Why do you think I'm so fat?"

"No, not fat. Never fat. Look at you, you're beautiful."

"That's not what he says. He promises me there will be no more babies. He hates me because I am a cow."

"No."

"Come sit by me on the sofa. Put your legs over the arm and lean back with your head in my lap. Touch my other breast. Milk me."

Before he disappears once more into his milky dream, he smells something new — the deep, mysterious smell of her womanhood, still hidden in nylon and leather, reaches out to him. Before he can find out what it is, she pulls his mouth to her other nipple, moans and sends him back to the secret place they have made together. All too soon this breast too is empty, his stomach is full and he sinks from this dream into the sleep he denied himself all night, his head falling against her lap.

She strokes his hair and pats him, content for now to let him sleep and renew himself as her breasts, empty now and just a little cold as their damp nakedness is left exposed, themselves begin to renew and refill.

He dreams a different dream now. His desperate desire for milk was the only thing in the world for so long, he had been unable to imagine anything more. Now that need is satisfied; not for the moment, but forever. And yet he isn't satisfied. In his new dream he is chasing something, something dark, a shadow, something he can't quite see but feels he has to catch. He wakes with a start, his face slick and sweating where it has rested against the leather of her skirt. She sees that he is upset and reaches to comfort him as she would her baby. Her breasts have begun to fill again, and she lifts one of them for him, ready to give him what she has, to soothe and comfort him, but he wrinkles up his face and fusses, just as her baby will sometimes do. He turns over, as if to return to sleep, and buries his face in her skirt.

He smells the leather and is wide awake again. He opens his eyes, but all he can see is black, the black leather of her skirt, just like the dark shadow that he chased in his dream. His mouth is wet and a little saliva drips out as he opens it to lick the leather, taste it, chew it. But the leather isn't what he dreamed of. Now he smells her, through the leather, and knows that what he smells is what has replaced the dream of milk. He wants it as he has never wanted anything, and he begins to bite and chew, trying to get through the leather at what is hidden underneath.

She puts her hands on his shoulders and pulls him hard against her, her back arching. She makes a long, low sound that isn't a word, and pulls harder on his shoulders as if to pull his whole body inside her. He loses his balance and slips from the sofa onto the floor, losing touch with her for a moment. Again he is on his knees. She puts her feet on his shoulders and sets her knees apart. The stockings end at her thighs, with a white lace belt above to hold them up. Nothing at all separates him from her open center.

The smell of her is overpowering. It is new to him, strange, but familiar somehow. The dream of milk is very far away. Her legs are dark where the nylon covers them, pale and smooth at the thighs, and where they meet is a dark, heavy tangle of hair. In the middle of this tangle are her lips, slightly parted and shining with moisture. That is where the smell comes from, and that is where he has to be. He leans toward her slowly. She lifts her feet from his shoulders and lets him approach. He inhales slowly, savoring her smell, and then he is right in front of her and the smell fills him until he is the smell of her. And he kisses her, so softly that his lips barely brush hers, her hair just touches his cheeks. The moisture that clings to her is slightly cool from being exposed to the air.

As he kisses her he whimpers, and she grabs his hair and pulls it. He makes a louder noise and dives at her, no longer gentle. His tongue slides up and down across her open lips, lapping at her wetness, trying to swallow it, to swallow her. He reaches inside her with his tongue, wanting to go deeper, to reach her womb, to reach the woman inside her. His nose is pressed hard against her lips, his head rocks back and forth, inhaling her, and somewhere far away he can hear her cries and shouts, can feel her pulling hard against his hair. Something small and hard is pressed against his cheek as his head slides from side to side through her wetness, and his tongue goes looking for it. He kisses her, harder now, sucking against her soft wetness, his tongue flicking in and out, darting around looking for that small, hard spot, finding it, rubbing it. When he touches it her back flies up, her feet slam on the floor beside his shoulders and her pelvis rises in the air before him. He clings to her as to his life. She is standing now, her knees still wide apart, her hands pressing his face against her as she screams and falls back against the seat, panting.

The tip of his tongue continues to press and surround the little button of flesh, feeling it throb and tremble. His hands are on her hips, and he can feel the trembling spread from where he kisses her to every part of her body. The tiny quiver against his mouth is a shaking in her hips, a heaving of her chest and shoulders and a wild thrashing of her arms. Her breasts are bouncing wildly and her cries have joined in a long, deep, guttural scream that rises and sinks and ends in a faraway sigh. He presses into her again, and she spasms again all over, wails, trembles, goes limp. Pleasure has become pain, and she slams her legs shut around his head to make him stop. His tongue retreats and instead he showers her with little kisses, sliding his lips, his nose, his cheeks back and forth in her slick darkness, laughing.

He finally is able to pull himself away from the warmth and softness, and looks up at her, smiling. She is smiling too, but tears are silently streaming down her face. She puts her hands under his shoulders and lifts his face to hers. As they kiss, she places her hand on his waist, slides it down and finds him hard and straining toward her. She runs her hand up and down against the cloth that holds him back, and his legs become weak again. He sinks onto the cushions, and their eyes finally meet on a level. She knees in front of him, and as she touches him again the image from his dream becomes clear, the shadow slips away and he knows what he was chasing.

He starts again to laugh, at himself. Here he is, twenty years old. What kind of fog has he been wondering in for . . . what, years now, that he should be surprised now at his own clear, simple desire? Where has he been for so long? And what great luck has brought him here now?

She has stepped back from him and he isn't sure why, until he, too, hears a sound in the hallway. No one ever comes here but the two of them — and the third, her husband. She looks alarmed.

"He has never come home in the daytime. Never. Go back through the rooms. Some of the doors still work. Just try them."

She kisses him hastily and pushes him through the door to the next room. Before he can turn and find out where he is he can hear her opening the windows in the first room, and no matter what the danger he can't help laughing again. How could she get the smell out of the room? It seems to him the whole world is full of her scent.

But he must find his way out. He is in a small, narrow room, almost like a hallway. He tries the first door he sees. It's locked. The knob won't even turn. He quickly moves on to the next. Here is the baby, sleeping peacefully. He has only heard it the one time. It certainly must be a happy baby with such a mother, spending most of its day in the peaceful dream of milk. He steps up to the crib and pats the child. It starts to stir and fuss, and suddenly less bold he hurries into the next room. It is the bedroom of the couple, dominated by a great, heavy canopy bed. He hesitates a moment. He doesn't want to leave. He wants her to join him, right now, under that canopy, and soothe the ache that has settled in his middle as his hardness, undiminished by fear or flight, begs him to finish what he has begun. Should he hide here and hope the husband leaves again at once? He hurries on. He passes through two more rooms outfitted with chairs, desks, tables, and wonders why they have bothered with so much furniture, as no one ever comes to see them. How can two people use so much space? He realizes he must be quite far from the door the man entered through by now, and he begins to try the doors which he thinks must join the hall, with no success. Still the rooms go on.

Soon, though, there is no more furniture. He passes through three rooms that are filled with boxes of all shapes and sizes. The man is certainly in the black market, as she said, and not shy about living with the evidence. Teams of men must have been needed to bring in so many things, and yet he has never noticed anything. Such a fog I have been living in. And then a door opens for him, and he is back in the plain hall of his floor, quite near his own door.

It is another sleepless night. He isn't afraid. What has happened to him has stirred something very deep in him that will never really rest again. His luck has been so absolute he feels that it will protect the woman as well, and tomorrow she will come for him and they will finish his education, his awakening. All night he can hear the coming and going of many feet, and he smiles. This must go on every night, and I never hear anything. Remarkable.

The long night fades away at last, but still he waits. It has been silent for hours, but surely it is best to wait until she comes. Finally he can wait no longer, and opens his door. From where he is, he can see the door to her apartment, standing open, and on the sill of his door are two things. The first is a folded paper. He picks it up, unfolds it and reads:

"I have no time. My husband thinks the police know where he is. He is taking us away. I don't know where. You are a beautiful young man. Remember me."

He still doesn't know her name. The other object is a small jar full of milk.

FIVE DIMES

Anita "Melissa"
Mashman

"You want me to do what?" I asked, surprised, looking down at the silver coins on my naked stomach.

Patiently he explained again.

"Stand in the middle of the room, with your legs spread. Then put your hands together, over your head, palm to palm, with a dime between each pair of fingers and your thumbs."

Pulse beating fast, I thought, *what interesting, little game does he have in mind this time?* I looked at the cheshire grin on his face and said:

"Anything you say, Lover."

I walked across the bare wooden boards where he had rolled up the fluffy rug and stood, legs spread, nipples tightening with excitement as I wondered what he had planned. I carefully balanced a dime on the tip of each finger and the thumb of my left hand. Then I put my right hand over the left, fingertip to fingertip, and raised my arms over my head. He took his time walking over to me, although his erection advertised that he was excited, too. He put one hand on my waist and began to walk around me slowly as he explained.

"No matter what I do, no matter how you feel, don't let go of the dimes."

He was behind me now, his left arm wrapped around my waist and his right hand lifting the long hair from my neck. He whispered in my ear:

"If you drop a dime, and you can be sure I'll hear it on this wooden floor, everything stops . . . everything."

Then he kissed my neck and nibbled on my ear, as his hands caressed my breasts. I moaned in dismay. Already my hands were sweaty. He kissed my neck more, sucking, nibbling, as his hands teased my tight nipples. He stepped back a bit and ran his nails lightly over my back, tracing tickling, exciting patterns, moving teasingly near my sensitive armpits. I shook with the effort to keep my arms up, when every nerve screamed for me to protect myself from being tickled. He stepped in front of me again, standing almost nose to nose, as his hands rested lightly, high on my sides.

"Nervous?" he asked, barely moving his fingers as I shivered.

"Please don't . . ." My plea hung in the air, unfinished, as his hands slid down my round stomach and between my legs, where my swollen labia dripped moisture.

"Well, somebody's excited," he said and softly stroked

my vaginal lips. I felt a tightening in my lower stomach, almost painful, as I responded, tilting my pelvis forward, desperately holding the slippery dimes above my head. He bent his head and sucked on my nipple, flicking it with his tongue as his fingers stroked and burrowed in my hot, wet cunt. My knees trembled and my arms shook with strain, but I held on to those five coins. I could feel moisture running down my leg, sweat or sexual fluids, I didn't know. His lips left my breast and he glanced up at my shaking arms and my equally shaky grin.

"Good girl," he said and kissed me, our tongues meeting and dancing. The fingers of his right hand rubbed gently round and round my clitoris. Then his left hand slithered down my sweaty back, between my buttocks, and gently stroked my anus, too. I almost came then, fingers rigid, thinking I would just die if I dropped a dime.

Abruptly he stopped, moving directly in front of me, his hands on my hips.

"No, no," I pleaded, "don't stop, please. I haven't dropped any coins."

I pushed my throbbing crotch against his stiff, satiny erection, wanting him to be as aroused as I was. My lover just smiled, sank to his knees and began to kiss my labia, teasingly. I closed my eyes, trying not to let the growing heat weaken my grip, as he gently parted my vaginal lips.

"Oh yes," I breathed as his tongue touched my clitoris. Tremors began in my thighs and I came then, crying out, as he took a long, sucking bite.

The dimes fell in a silvery shower as my exhausted arms fell forward, and I caressed my lover's head.

Slowly, I calmed down, my knees felt stronger, the cramps left my fingers. I bent over, picked up the dimes and put them in my lover's hand.

"Your turn," I whispered in his ear.

IN GRIFF'S IN L.A. ON A RAINY SUNDAY AFTERNOON IN FEBRUARY

Carter Wilson

•

... there was this guy. Six foot, big shoulders, black shirt, black jeans, boots, leather jacket, short black stubble beard, heavy. A Blutto, Italian-gangster look, broad nose, big dark eyebrows, full lips. He was giving me glances and at first I was smiling at him but then looking away or walking the other direction. Then I saw him closer up, and even in the dark I could tell he was classically, nature's-aristocrat ugly, and hot. Finally he was standing next to me in the crowd and I turned and was about to go, but instead I said something like, "Hard getting by here," and he said, "Um," and then asked me my name.

George.

His was Bernie, he said. You from around here?

Santa Cruz. Ever come up that way?

My family used to always spend the summer there, he said. We were from over in the Valley.

Where?

Outside Manteca. Last times I've been through Santa Cruz it was hard to find a room there under a hundred dollars.

We were standing right up against each other, other guys pushing past, and I began smelling him. Either his sweat or his wet leather jacket's smell or the two together. Bernie was very lightly playing his hand along the outside of my pants, touching where my dick was. Very light rubbing, hardly there, until my dick began to get hard. He backed off and then he touched it again and I shoved it back up against him.

What do you do?

I'm an assistant branch manager for World.

You hold the mortgage on my house.

Yeah? Well, we hold a lot of them.

I felt around for his cock and found it. A nice little mound in the assistant branch manager's pants.

OK to unbutton you?

Go ahead.

He had on no underwear. I felt flesh and crotch hair right away. Then something else hard.

What you got in here, Bernie?

There's a two inch stretcher around my balls.

That's what it was, a cuff of leather with two big-headed metal fasteners and a ring on its underside. I felt Bernie's nuts below the cuff, hard, forced together, smooth under the taut skin. I snuck my finger into the ring and tugged a little. That what this is for? I whispered up close to his ear.

Yeah. Or for hanging weights on.

How long you been wearing this thing?

Put it on about two hours ago. There's a Prince Albert down there too.

What's that?

A ring through my cock.

I felt again. Bernie's dick was small and cut and not getting particularly hard. There was a metal ring pierced through the flesh of the head, held with little metal balls. I took him around the corner outside in the half light by the shed and spit in my palm and rubbed it against his nuts where they were exposed.

That feel good?

Yes it does.

I undid my zipper and got the fly of my underpants spread open for him. Almost immediately he started getting his finger up under my foreskin. He told me he wished he could get me off some place and blow me. I tugged his tee shirt up and thumbed his nipples and plucked at them and then felt the soft roll of flesh around his belly.

What you weigh, Bernie?

About 250.

And your whole body's smooth like this?

81

Except for my legs. And my ass. For some reason there's a lot of hair in the crack of my ass.

And you like foreskin?

Foreskin drives me crazy.

I kissed him. Bernie kept his mouth small and let me run my tongue inside. Sweet in there.

Would you ever show your ass off to someone you liked?

I'd be glad to.

I asked if it could ever be spanked and he said by the right guy, sure.

I told him my lover was in the bar with me and he said he had a lover too. They'd been together three years, this was the first time they'd ever gone out separately. I said maybe we could try some kind of three-way thing, but he said he'd tried that in the past and it'd never worked out for him.

Later, when Doug and I were getting ready to leave, I noticed Bernie standing by the door so I asked would he step outside with me so I could get a look at him in better light. He put his drink down on the bar and came with me.

I had been right. He was really beautiful.

How old are you? I said.

Forty. Why?

No reason, I said. I asked had it hurt having his cock pierced. He said the piercing itself not so bad but the first time afterward that he tried to pee he had thought he was going to pass out from the pain. Like having salt poured on it, he said.

❋   ❋   ❋

And later still, jacking off thinking about the kind of blowjob
Bernie would give, I also begin imagining some poor guy
leaning over the assistant branch manager's desk and mur-
muring, "You know you got me by the balls, mister," but
you and I know the kick is that it's really the World Savings
assistant manager whose pleasure it is to have *himself* by his
own pretty little tight nuts.

HORNY

Greg Boyd

·

I wake up horny. God's punishing me again, testing my endurance, so I fall to my knees and pray for strength. But evil thoughts course through my mind like a polluted stream. I try my best to purify them. I am chlorine, lava soap. I bubble and foam, but in the end it happens again anyway. It's always the same. My soul screams at the exact moment of my body's release. It's a righteous voice that wells up inside me, a deep and hoary voice that comes out of the wilderness and is filled with the indignation of the ages. It inspires in me a kind of holy terror and afterwards I shake for a good five minutes.

Though I won't eat today, I allow myself one cup of instant coffee. Then I go into the garage and give myself fifty lashes on my bare back with a leather strap. Afterwards I climb up on a stepladder and take down the cross I keep suspended from the rafters. I built it myself from heavy lumber, wood screws and angle braces I bought at the hardware store. I had to carry the beams six miles home with me in two separate trips because they wouldn't fit in or on my car. That was months ago, back when I still had a car. It was mid-summer then, and under the sun's whip the sweat dripped from my vile body as I walked and melted my impure thoughts about beach girls in their bikinis. I was already learning how to suffer.

There are leather straps on the cross for me to hold onto so that I can keep it balanced as I walk. The first few times I used it I kept dropping it on the sidewalk and by the end of the day my hands were full of splinters from trying to catch ahold of it when it started to slip from off my shoulder. Like I said, it's a very heavy cross, and long enough so that if it were put into the ground, and raised up on end with me nailed to it like it's supposed to be, it would still be plenty high to keep me way above everyone so they could see just how much I'm suffering up there. The splinters were actually never a problem, as they only added to my suffering and my contemplation thereof as I pulled them out with tweezers at home later, and it's nice for the cross to hit the sidewalk once in a while, where it makes a huge noise, though better, I think, for me to fall with it, to one knee or even right onto my face, which happens more often now that I'm actually strapped to it, but once a woman with a baby carriage was walking past me and I kind of leaned over a bit to look at her and just as I was getting a good peek the cross started to slip and only the grace of God spared her child, though the carriage was damaged beyond repair. Praise be to God.

Since then the police have kept close tabs on me. It was even their idea to use the leather hand straps. They've given me a few simple guidelines to follow as well. It's a free country, they tell me, but I'm not to bother people. And they've asked me to stay out of the mall, which is where I had a little trouble another time on account of the over-zealous security officers there who accused me of disturbing with my wild stares and weird cross the young girl–shoppers that mill around eating salted pretzels and sucking orange drinks through straws. The security guards wanted to grab my arms and guide me forcibly to the exit and when I refused to let them abuse my rights to freedom of religion and expression they ended up calling the police to have me arrested for disorderly conduct and disrupting the peace. Except for those two times the police have been nice enough whenever they stop their cars to check in with me along the sidewalk downtown, and there's even a young lady officer who wears her tight blue uniform shirt with the badge pinned right over her swelling chest, though none of them can keep themselves from winking at each other or chuckling. They know I'm not a criminal, but, even so, they still like to imagine I'm some kind of kook. But that laugh-about-it-all attitude is understandable given all the wickedness and depravity they witness on a daily basis.

I strip down completely and wrap the loincloth I made from an old white sheet between my legs and then twice around my waist. It's modest but authentic. I fasten it tightly at both the waist and legs with safety pins to keep the cloth from falling down and my private parts from spilling out as I grapple with the cross. I won't stand for people having any lewd thoughts or fantasies about an act that's meant to purify. And I certainly don't want to be humiliated in public. Outside I hear the wind blowing rain against the garage door as I get ready. No doubt about it, today I'm going to suffer.

On the street I see one of my neighbors, dressed in a yellow plastic raincoat, stooping to pick up her newspaper. She waves to me briefly before she scurries back inside her house, even though she knows I can't wave back because my hands are holding onto the wet straps of the cross. She's an attractive young woman who works in an office. Sometimes I see her getting out of her car in the evening, her tight skirt riding up her thighs, her high heels gleaming in the late afternoon light. Only recently married, she and her husband have lived on my street just a few months. For a second I catch a glimpse of her legs as she stoops, and I wonder what, if anything, she's wearing under the raincoat. Even at this distance I can tell that her breasts are full and round. Her big red nipples puff out and stand erect beneath the cold plastic, begging for my tongue's devotion. Her hot host is already moist with the anticipation of everlasting joy, of paradise on earth, of things to come.

But God loves me. My thoughts are interrupted by a car at the corner that splashes the cold and holy water of repentance upon me as it passes through a puddle in the road, drenching my budding lust in its wake. My hair clings limply to my head and rainwater runs down my face as I struggle against the weight of the cross, the cold, the wind that sends chilling spikes of pain up and down my legs. Sharp pebbles press into my bare feet. I pass through residential neighborhoods and as I do I know that temptation lurks behind every door, every window. I avert my eyes, cast them downward. Along the sidewalk I see drowned earthworms that have been flushed like so many unclean corpses out from their soaked graves. Bent beneath my burden I contemplate my life and its eventual end. As the sky weeps, so do I, for my sins are great and many.

Downtown I walk past rows of storefronts, windows full of worldly goods. I don't let myself look inside or think about the shopgirls standing in their short skirts — how they pull their pantyhose up over their long legs in the morning, how they push their firm breasts into the cups of their lacy bras, how they splash perfume behind their ears and knees in anticipation. Finally I take my position at the center of town, stand silently in the rain at the intersection of Broadway and Main. People drive past in their warm, dry cars, listening to pop songs about love, or more often about love-making — the words barely clothed in a fine, see-through mesh of metaphor that leaves little to the imagination. Some of them honk their horns at me. Perhaps they know me. In better weather they might speak to me, offer me their blessing or ask for mine. More likely they recognize what I represent, why I am here. They understand that safe inside their cars they are swimming in filthy thoughts, vile debauchery.

A man and a woman in a blue Mercedes drive past slowly, staring at me *with unbelieving eyes*. The man wears an expensive suit, the woman a silk blouse under a tweed blazer. No doubt they've just come from a motel where they've been engaging in every illicit sex-act conceivable. No doubt his penis now hangs between his legs swollen red, bruised and sore from pounding inside her tight and hungry hole. No doubt her vagina likewise feels ragged and sore from their debauch, its soft walls stretched and battered from the satanic thrashing action of the devil's massive, oversized piston. It takes a long time for the car to turn the corner, an eternity. All the while the woman looks into my eyes, first through the hysterical waving arms of the windshield wipers, then, head turned sharply to the side, through the passenger window, a harlot, a fellow sinner in need of spiritual guidance, pleading for help, for compassion. I am here for her, a beacon set firmly in place in the midst of a storm. I loosen my hand from its tether to signal and the cross slips, pulling me with it to the wet concrete. When I touch my face, my hand comes away bloody. She is gone.

I could have saved her. I could have taught her how to love. I could have taken her by the hand. I could have undressed her with my teeth. I could have . . .

By the time I get home it's nearly dark. I'm soaked to the bone, skin blue and shrivelled, feet numb and bloody, chilled, shivering, feverish. I wrap one towel around my head, another around my shoulders, a third over my legs and sit in front of the television for hours drinking hot tea and watching cable network evangelism. The first hour features a fiery preacher who explains the sufferings of Jesus for Mankind while threatening me with eternal damnation and a gospel rock singer with lips made for fellatio. Later, before my very eyes a blind woman has her vision restored by the love of Christ and a cripple walks when he accepts the Lord as his personal savior. As the camera pans the audience to show the radiant faces of the true believers I see a pretty woman in the third row that I want to fuck. I am exalted, mesmerized, shivering uncontrollably.

At eleven o'clock I switch off the television and pray on stiff knees in total darkness for an hour and a half. I go to bed exhausted and hopelessly horny.

ME AND THE BOYS

Trish Thomas

•

I don't know what's up with me and boys lately, but alla the sudden I want one. Not just any boy, a faggot. And not just any faggot, a drag queen. And not just any drag queen, Dreamboat. It's crazy how this shit works, but sometimes, outta the blue, my cunt starts doing my thinking for me because my brain can't handle what my cunt is telling me to do. That's how this whole thing with Dreamboat got started.

There we were one ordinary day, hanging out, drinking coffee and smoking cigarettes like usual, when I got up to go take a piss. Right when I got back to the table he stood up to go himself and bam, I was frozen in time. My pussy started humming and for a split second I wasn't aware of anything except the length of his body, right in front of mine, and the fact that I suddenly wanted to grab him and pull him against me. From my head down to my toes, I was on fire. It didn't show on my face, I made sure of that, and he went on to the bathroom without any idea that I came *this close* to slam-dunking him right there on the table in the middle of the coffee shop.

I sat down and lit a cigarette. By the time he got back to the table I was normal again. Naturally I didn't mention my flash of desire for him because he's a faggot and I'm a dyke, and my brain was back in control, and my cunt can't talk.

I tried to put it outta my head but now I was looking at Dreamboat in a whole new way. Every time I'd see him after that I wanted to jump his bones. Not only that, but I started having alla these dreams about him. The dreams were pure mush. All we ever did was make out and hold hands. It got so I was embarrassed to wake up in the morning. So embarrassed that I've been forced to develop full-blown daytime fantasies just to save face. Fantasies that range from clandestine, passionate kissing up against the walls of public bathrooms to putting a leather horse-bit in his mouth and pulling back on the reins while I fist him from behind, doggy style, on the kitchen floor of his apartment, where his roommates could walk in and bust us at any moment.

Then *that* started freaking me out too. *What's a nice butch dyke like me doing fantasizing about a drag queen with a dick?* But you know, so few people really turn me on that it seems kinda silly to get hung up on a gender thing. Besides, if I fuck him, I'll still be a dyke because that's what I am. Simple. I don't want him the way a woman wants a man. I don't

even want him the way a fag hag wants a fag. I want him
the way a perverted, horny bulldagger wants a young, tender
drag queen in a tight black slip and combat boots, which is
what he had on the day he *really* took me over the edge. The
day my brain said *fuck it* and gave in to my cunt. But that
came later. I'm getting ahead of myself. First, there was
Pretty Boy.

Now Pretty Boy is actually a *girl*. Not in the way that
*Dream*boat is a girl. Pretty Boy is a girl with a pussy. A girl
who *looks* like a 15-year-old boy, so naturally I was attracted
to her right off.

By the time I took her home I was way overdue. I hadn't
picked up a girl since I quit drinking. Forgot how. Plus
which, the idea of being caught naked in the same room with
another human being, without the help of 5 or 6 kamikazes,
scared the living shit out of me. It was starting to look like
I was never gonna fuck again, but I refused to give up. One
night, I did it.

Bolstered by sheer horniness, I think about what I want and
scan the crowded bar to see who can give it to me. Not the
blond, too femme and too innocent, she wouldn't know what
to do with me. Not the girl with the overgrown mohawk
who's leaning against the wall. Too wasted. She'd probably
pass out before we even got going good. I know how that
goes. And not the one who just planted herself in front of
me. No pizazz. No edge. No challenge.

Her. Up on stage. Wrapping up the mic cords from the

band that just finished playing. She's shorter than me and smaller, but she looks sturdy. I bet she can hold her own. I move closer to get a better look. She's got a boy's hands and a boy's torso. No breasts that I can see. She's wearing a *Thrasher* T-shirt and faded black jeans that hang loose on her hips. Her hair is short and messy. She looks like she just got outta bed. I wonder if she got fucked right before she came to work.

She looks up and sees me staring at her. We've talked before but this is different and she knows it. She can tell from the smug expression on my face and the angle of my head that I've already looked her up and down, assessing her. I don't approach her. I give her time to think about my silent offer and decide what she wants to do. It doesn't surprise me when she comes over later and sits down next to me.

A mixture of shit and lube drips down from her asshole onto my thigh. She's on her knees. Her face is smashed into the pillow. Her wrists lay still in the small of her back, bound by leather restraints and locked together by a snaphook that's attached to a long chain that runs over the base of her spine, down between her legs, up under her belly, between her tits and up to her throat where it stops, padlocked to the leather dog collar that she wears around her neck. Each time she rears her head and bucks up against me, the chain pulls tighter across her cunt.

I'm sitting behind her on the bed. Her ass is marked with

my fingerprints from the night before, inches away from my face, right under my nose. I'm working a butt plug into her asshole and pumping a dildo in and out of her cunt. I'm mesmerized by the smell of her and the rhythm of fucking.

I leave the butt plug in place and put my hand up to her mouth. She pulls off the latex glove with her teeth and I throw it on the floor with the others. We've been going at it for 3 days, stopping only to eat and sleep and piss and shit.

I pick up a leather paddle and start smacking her hard on the ass, alternating sides, while I keep pumping the dildo into her pussy. The sharp stinging that rushes through her torso really gets her going. When she's finally finished cumming, I ease the plug out of her asshole. It's caked with shit. I slide the dildo out of her cunt. It's covered with blood. I snap the hook off of her restraints, bring her hands up to the top of her head, and lay them on the pillow. I lay on top of her and grind my pelvis against her hips. The clean cock that's strapped over my pussy slides in and out between her thighs.

"I want you to suck me off."

She turns over onto her back and sits up. I've lost all track of time and become aware of the rising sun only because the light coming through my bedroom window lets me see how red her lips are as she closes them around the cock. I love watching her do this to me just like I love watching her eat. The way she opens her mouth with no hesitation every time I offer her food from my plate. Hungry. And willing.

I reach behind her head and pull hard on her hair, just to see her mouth fall open. I push her face into my crotch.

I rock back and forth on my knees, fucking her open mouth. Underneath the harness, my clit gets hard. The inside of my cunt is soaking wet. I'm getting ready to cum but I don't wanna cum like this. Some butches are too butch to spread their legs; I'm too butch not to.

"I want you to fuck me."

I unbuckle the harness and pull it out of the crack of my ass. She slips it on over her own thighs while I turn around and put my ass in her face. She lubes the cock and holds it in her hand, rubbing its tip up and down my cunt from behind. I think I'm gonna pass out if she doesn't give it to me soon.

"Fuck me, you bitch."

That's what she was waiting for. She shoves it all the way inside me with one easy thrust. I can see us in the mirror that's at the head of my bed. *Jesus we look good.* She gets a grip on my thighs and pushes the cock deeper into my cunt. She fucks me for what seems like forever. *Jesus god this is good.* I cum once like this but I'm not done yet.

"I want your fist."

She pulls out and I turn over. She reaches behind me and takes two gloves out of the box on the headboard, puts one on each hand, and smears them with lube. She lifts my legs into the air and slips her thumb into my asshole. My eyes close, my back raises off the bed, and my muscles loosen to take her in.

I open my eyes and watch her face while she gives my cunt one finger, two fingers, three fingers, all four fingers. Just like that. Even though she's done this to me many times already, she's still amazed by the size of my pussy. She winces when she gives me her whole fist. She can't believe I take it so easily. I don't move. I'm savoring the feeling of being completely full with this fag girl's hand.

I plant my feet on the bed and push my hips up to her. Now I want it hard. She uses her whole body to give it to me. I'm staring at her. Looking her right in the face while she takes my entire pussy with her hand drives me outta my fucking mind. I'm gone. I'm outta this world. Everything is outta focus. I've given myself over.

I pull her hand out of my asshole. She knows what I want. She leaves her fist in my pussy but stops stroking it. She slaps me in the face. My nipples get hard. I slap her back. I don't know why slapping the woman who's fucking me turns me on, but it does.

My hands drop down between my legs. She stops slapping me. She pushes her fist to the back of my cunt and starts stroking again. I push my hips against her and use my hands to work my swollen clit until I cum. When I do, she pulls her fist out real slow. She lies next to me on her side. I roll over and lay my belly against hers.

"I like what you look like when you're getting ready to cum."

"What do I look like?"

"Like an animal."

Me and Pretty Boy have been doing it for a few weeks now. She matches me fetish for fetish. What a lucky fucking break.

Still, I can't seem to shake this vision of riding Dreamboat from behind with the horse bit in his mouth and the reins in my hands. I want it all. I don't have the balls to hit on him. I'm used to getting what I want but frankly, I'm afraid I'm outta my league with this one. The guy's a faggot for christ sake. What if I come on to him and he laughs in my face? I don't know.

I don't know, but here I am at Sunny Leather and I got a little extra money in my pocket so I pick out a horse bit and take it to the counter along with a couple bottles of lube and a box of latex gloves. I'm waiting for my change and out of the corner of my eye I spot an empty pair of combat boots in the dressing room to my left. I get my change and back up, real casual, to the magazine rack behind me.

I pick up a magazine and pretend to leaf through it. The curtain on the dressing room is halfway open, from this angle I have a perfect view of the girl inside. Her back is toward me. Her legs are long and lean and slightly bowed. She's wearing black stockings with seams and a red garter belt. Her thighs are solid and curve sweetly into a nice, round ass. Her back spreads in a perfect V out to her broad shoulders. I can't see her face yet cuz she's pulling something on over her head.

Oh my god, it's Dreamboat. My pussy thumps.

He pulls a black satin slip over his hips and smooths out the hem. He turns to one side and then the other, admiring his profile in the mirror. My pussy starts to throb. He rubs his hand over his crotch and I can see his cock getting hard. He lifts up the front of his slip and starts to stroke it. I watch it get thicker and longer. My cunt has almost convinced me to go into the dressing room and have my way with him when the manager announces that the store is closing. Dreamboat stops what he's doing and strips. He shoves the stockings and lingerie into his pockets and walks out of the store.

Now, Dreamboat dressed like a boy is one thing. Dreamboat dressed in tacky drag is something else. But Dreamboat in a tight black satin slip with a stiff cock is a whole nother story. I follow him home.

He walks up to Market Street and heads for the underground. He's got on headphones and he's oblivious to everything around him, so he doesn't notice me. I wait till he's on the escalator before I put my Fast Pass in the slot and go through the gate. I walk down the stairs at the opposite end of the platform. We're the only two down here. He thinks he's alone and starts dancing around. I lean against the wall and watch him. I want him.

Three outbound cars come at once. He gets on the first one, I get on the last. From where I'm sitting I can watch all the doors and I see him get out at Castro Station. I follow him up to the street. I'm right behind him but he still has no idea he's being followed. He heads down Castro and goes into the Walgreen's. I drop back and pretend to look into the store windows while I wait for him. *Oh shit, there's Pretty Boy at the ATM.* I duck into a doorway and peek out. Pretty Boy walks away from the ATM and crosses the street in the middle of the block. She gets into her truck and starts the engine. *Whew. She didn't see me. Good.*

I look down the street just in time to spot Dreamboat coming out of Walgreen's carrying a small package. He crosses Castro and continues down 18th Street. I'm on his tail again. He makes a left at the next block onto his street. I lay back a little now. I stop to light a cigarette while he walks up the stairs to his flat. He puts his key in the lock, opens the door, and goes inside. I climb the stairs and try the door knob. It turns. *Excellent.* I open the door a crack and see him heading down the hall toward the kitchen. He stops at the bathroom and goes inside. I toss my cigarette over the railing and slip in the front door, closing it behind me. I step lightly down the hall to the bathroom. The door's open. He's standing in front of the toilet. He unsnaps his fly, pulls out his dick, and starts to piss. I come up behind him and drop my bag from Sunny Leather on the floor. My pelvis is on his ass. I put one hand over his mouth and the other hand under his dick.

"Don't move."

Not only doesn't he move, he stops pissing mid-stream. He's scared.

"Don't stop. Piss in my hand."

He does. I slip my hand under the bib of his overalls and wipe his piss on his chest.

"You always leave your front door unlocked?"

"Only when somebody's following me."

Son of a bitch. I turn him around and shove him against the wall.

"When did you first see me?"

His face turns red and he looks down at his feet.

100

"When I was in the dressing room. When you were pretending to read the magazine. Before I grabbed my dick."

He gets hard again when he tells me this. He looks up at me and smiles sheepishly.

I lean back against the sink and take a quick survey of the bathroom. An empty Fleet's enema box is in the trash. His pockets are bulging with stolen lingerie. The bag that he brought from Walgreen's is laying on the back of the toilet. I pick it up and look inside. Disposable razors.

"Getting ready for a night out?"

He blushes again. I open the pack of razors and take one out.

His dick starts to sway up and down and he takes a deep breath.

"Come on," I say, and I grab my bag and walk into the kitchen. I sit down on the table and prop my feet up on a chair. I lean forward, fold my hands, and rest my elbows on my knees. He's still standing in the doorway of the bathroom. I motion with my finger for him to come to me. He walks over and bends down to kiss me but I push him away. He looks at me, confused. I can see he's nervous and doesn't know what to do, so I tell him.

"I wanna see you in that shit you stole from the store."

He loosens up a little, now he's in familiar territory. He unhooks the straps on his overalls and lets them drop to the floor. He leans back against the refrigerator and pulls his boots off. He picks up the overalls and takes out the slip, the garter belt, and the stockings, and puts them all on. I stand up and offer him a cigarette and he leans forward gracefully for me to light it. A strap falls off his shoulder. Standing in front of me is six feet of white trash girl-boy with short blond hair and big, dark blue eyes, holding his cigarette like he's a society lady at a big-money cocktail party. Poised and delicate and dignified, he waits for me to tell him what to do next.

"Sit down."

He sits on the edge of the table.

I walk over to one of the cabinets and take out a big bowl. I carry it to the sink and fill it with warm water. I grab a towel and a bottle of soap and carry everything to the table. I put my hand on his chest and push him back, lift up his legs and spread em. I pull the slip up past his ass and lather the hair around his asshole. I take out two gloves and put them on. His dick starts swaying again when I pick up the razor. When I'm done shaving him, I wash him off with the warm water and dry him with the towel.

I grab the front of his slip and pull him up to me hard. Both of the straps snap and the slip falls down to his waist. I kiss him on the mouth slow and soft. He sucks on the ring on my bottom lip like it's a pacifier. I pull him down to the floor, still kissing him. I smear lube on one of my hands and pin him down while I slide two fingers into his asshole. He takes them both, no problem. I fuck him slow with two fingers for a while. He starts to moan and grabs his dick. I pour more lube on my hand and add my other two fingers, one at a time. I've got all four fingers in him and I'm fucking him a little faster now. He takes my hand off his chest and

102

pulls my fingers into his mouth like he's sucking a cock. *Sweet*.

I take my fingers out of his mouth and his asshole.

"Turn over."

While he's getting on all fours I take the horse bit out of the bag and lean over him to put it in his mouth. He bites down and I draw the leather reins behind his neck. I pull his head back so he's facing the ceiling while I move into his asshole again with my hand. He's panting. His head is in the air and his back is swayed. He rocks his ass into my hand. His asshole is open wide. The walls inside are smooth and wet with lube and some leftover shit that the enema didn't get. He's really moaning now and I work my thumb in alongside my fingers. His asshole opens wider and wider until my hand practically falls in. I'm in up to my wrist. I push in a little farther and his mouth drops open. I let go of the reins and the bit drops on the floor.

"Say my name."

He whispers it.

"Say it again, louder."

He says my name loud over and over again like he's in a trance. His voice keeps getting higher. It's late and it should be dark but there's a full moon tonight and I can see my arm pumping into his asshole. I've never fisted anybody in the ass before and it's an amazing feeling. Every time I slow down I can feel his pulse from inside and I gotta gasp for air. My pussy is throbbing for attention. He grabs his cock and starts jacking himself off. I can't see it but just thinking about his big, thick cock makes me wanna pull out my hand and flip him over before he cums and it's too late.

The kitchen light snaps on and floods the room. *Oh fuck. Not now.* I know in my fantasy I wanted Dreamboat's roommates to walk in and bust us but not any more. This is too sweet and too raw for an audience and I'm not ready to stop. I turn my head and look behind me. It's not his roommates, it's Pretty Boy. *Fuck.* Now what do I do? What's she gonna think seeing me kneeling on the kitchen floor behind Dreamboat with my arm halfway up his ass and him whinnying like a stallion?

I look back at Dreamboat who's shooting cum onto the floor. I look back at Pretty Boy again. She unbuttons her fly and her cock drops out. She pulls a rubber out of her pocket and rolls it up the cock. *Excellent.*

TWO AT ONCE

Robert Silverberg

•

"You never have?" Louise asked. "Not ever?"

This was in the glorious seventies, when everyone was doing everything to everyone, in every imaginable combination. I was young, healthy, prosperous and single. And we were in Los Angeles, city of year-round summer and infinite possibility.

"Not even once," I said. "Things just haven't clicked the right way, I guess."

"Well," Louise said, "let me think about this."

What we were discussing — over Belgian waffles and mimosas at a favorite breakfast place of mine on the Sunset Strip — was my primo fantasy, the one sexual act — well, not the only one, but the only one that really interested me — that I had never managed to experience: making love to two women at the same time. Fucking one, amiably caressing the other, then switching, then maybe resting for a little while and watching as they amused each other, and then starting the whole cycle again, Ms. A. followed by Ms. B — the good old sandwich game, me as the filling, double your pleasure, double your fun —

Louise sipped her mimosa and thought about it. Her brow furrowed; her wheels were turning.

"Janet?" she said. "No. No, that won't work. Martine? Probably not. Kate?" She shook her head. Then: "Dana, maybe?"

It was maddening. Delicious possibilities flickered one by one in her eyes, rose briefly to the level of a bright gleam, and died away with a shake of her head just as each of the girls she named started to assume a thrilling reality in my mind. I had no more idea who Janet was, or Kate or Martine, than you do. They were only names to me; but for the single dazzling instant that they dangled in the air between us as potential members of our trio they were glorious names already turning into delectable flesh, and in the hyperactive arena of my imagination I could see myself rolling around in bed with lovely Louise and lissome Janet (blonde, leggy, slim-hipped) or luscious Louise and languid Martine (dark ringlets, heavy swaying breasts) or lascivious Louise and lubricious Kate (bright sparkling eyes, tiny tattoo on left buttock). But as fast as the tantalizing visions arose, Louise dismissed them. Janet had moved to San Francisco, she remembered now; Martine was in a relationship; Kate's motorcycle had gone into a ditch in Topanga Canyon the week

before. Bim, bam, boom: all three vanished from my life just
like that and I had never even known them.

"Dana, though," she said. Louise's eyes brightened again
and this time they stayed that way. "Yes. Yes. Very probably
a yes. Let me see what I can do about Dana, all right?"

"Dana's a female?" I asked uneasily.

Louise giggled. "For Christ's sake, Charlie, what do you
think?"

"I knew a Dana in college once. A man."

"You said two women, didn't you? Come on, then." She
tossed me a mischievous look. "Unless it's the other kind of
threesome you were thinking of."

"Not exactly, Louise."

"I wouldn't mind that, you know."

"I bet you wouldn't. But I would."

"Well, then. All right." She winked. "I'll see what I can
manage."

A hot little quiver of anticipation ran through me. Louise
would manage something: I was sure of it. This was the
giddy seventies, after all, when the whole planet was in heat.
We were in Los Angeles, global capital of carefree copulation.
And Louise, slim, agile, raven-haired, uninhibited Louise,
was very resourceful indeed. She made her living setting
up window displays for the innumerable little women's-
clothing boutiques that had sprouted up all over Venice
and Santa Monica and West Hollywood, and she knew
hundreds of women models, fitters, designers and boutique
owners, nearly all of whom were young, attractive and
single.

"Finish your mimosa," Louise said. "Let's go to the beach."

Louise did her window work between three in the afternoon and half past eight at night. Plenty of time for play, before or after.

"Isn't it too cool today?" I asked.

"The radio says it'll be seventy-five degrees by ten o'clock."

January 13th. Seventy-five degrees. I love L.A. in the winter. We went to the beach: the old nude beach at To-panga, the one they closed down around 1980 when the people in the expensive beach houses began to get tired of the show. The water was a little chilly, so all we did was run ankle-deep into the surf and quickly out again, but the beach itself was fine. We basked and chatted and built a sand castle — more of a bungalow, really — and around noon we got dressed and drove down to Louise's place in Venice to shower away the sand. Of course we took the shower together and one thing led to another, and between that and lunch Louise was a little late getting to work. Nobody would mind.

We were such good friends, Louise and I. We had known each other for three years and at least once a week, usually on a Tuesday or Wednesday morning, we had breakfast together and went to the beach. Then we went to her place and balled. We liked each other's company. Neither of us expected anything more than that from the other: company. She was twenty-eight; I was a couple of years older. Good friends, yes. I had met her at a bookshop on Melrose and we had liked each other right away and there we were. We didn't give a thought about getting married, either to each other or anyone else. What a nice decade that was! The stock market went to hell, the government was a mess, inflation was fifteen percent, sometimes you had to wait on line for an hour and a half to buy gas. But for Louise and me and a lot of others like us it was the time of our lives. Yes. The time of our lives. Everybody young, everybody single, and we were going to stay that way forever.

Two days later she called me and asked, "Are you free Saturday night?"

"I could be." We rarely saw each other on weekends. "Why?"

"I talked to Dana."

"Oh," I said. "Well, then!"

"Will you spring for dinner for three at Le Provence?"

"I could do that, yes." Le Provence was a small and very authentic French restaurant in Westwood that we liked. Dinner for three would run me close to forty bucks in the quaint money of the era, a nice bottle of wine included. But I could afford it. I was writing continuity for Saturday morning TV then — Captain Goofus and His Space Brigade. Don't laugh. Captain Goofus kept me solvent for four seasons and some residuals, and I miss him very much. "Tell me about Dana," I said.

"New York girl. Been here about a year. Medium tall, brown hair, glasses, nice figure, very bright. Smokes. You mind that?"

"I can survive. Stacked?"

"Not especially. But she's built okay."

"How do you know her?"

"She's a customer at Pleasure Dome on Santa Monica. Came into the store one night in November while I was setting up the Christmas window. We've had lunch a few times."

"You sure she'll go for this, Louise?"

"Le Provence, Saturday night, half past seven, okay?"

My first blind date in years. Well, all right. Louise vouched for her. The two of them were already there, sitting at a table in the back, when I showed up at the restaurant. In half a minute I knew that things were going to work out. Dana was around twenty-five, slender, pleasant-looking if unspectacular, with big horn-rimmed glasses and quick, penetrating eyes. Her whole vibe was New York: alert, intelligent, fearless. Ready to throw herself joyously into our brave new California world of healthy, anything-goes erotic fun. I didn't sense any tremendous pheromonal output coming from her that related specifically to *me*, no instantaneous blast of lust, just a generalized willingness to go along with the project. But that was okay. We had only just met, after all. Expecting a woman to fall down instantly at my feet foaming with desire has never been any prerequisite of mine: simple willingness is quite sufficient for me.

My ever-active mind began to spin with fantasies. I saw myself sprawled out on the big water bed with Louise to my left and Dana to my right, all of us naked, both of them pressing close against me, squirming and wriggling. I imagined the sleek texture along the inside of Dana's thighs and the feel of her cool firm breasts against my hands while the rest of me was busy with Louise. And then slipping free of Louise and turning to Dana, gliding into her up to the hilt while Louise hovered above us both, grazing my back with the tips of her breasts —

Back in the real world Dana and I started to make polite first-date chitchat, with Louise sitting there beaming like a matchmaker whose clients are going in the right direction.

"So, Louise tells me you write for television?"

"Saturday morning cartoons. Captain Goofus and His Space Brigade."

"Far out! You must make a mint."

"Half a mint, actually. It's not bad. And you?"

"A word processor," she said.

"A what?"

"Typist, sort of. Except I use a kind of computer, you know? In a law office in Beverly Hills?"

I didn't know. Computers were something very new then.

"Must be movie lawyers," I said. "They're the only ones who can afford a gadget like that."

She named the firm. Entertainment law, all right. But actually Dana wanted to write screenplays; the word-processing thing was just a way station en route to success. I smiled. This city has always been full of ambitious would-be screenwriters, two-thirds of them from New York. I expected her to pull a script out of her purse any minute. But Dana wasn't that tacky. The conversation bubbled on, and somewhere along the way we ordered, and I felt so up about the whole thing that I selected a nine-dollar bottle of Bordeaux. Nine dollars was a lot for a bottle of wine in those days.

We'd be done with dinner by nine, I figured, and it was a five-minute drive over to my apartment on Barrington just above Wilshire, and figure half an hour for some drinks, brandy or sherry or whatever, and a little music and soft lights and a couple of joints — this was the seventies, remember — and the clothes would begin to come off, and then the migration to the water bed —

Two women at once, at last! My dream fulfilled!

But then a waitress we hadn't noticed up till then brought the wine to the table and things started to go strange.

She was standing next to me, going through her elaborate bottle-opening rigmarole, cutting the red seal and inserting the corkscrew and all, paying all the attention to me because obviously I was the one who would be picking up the bill, when suddenly she happened to glance toward Dana and I heard her gasp.

"Oh, my *God!* Dana! What are *you* doing in L.A.?"

Dana hadn't looked at the waitress at all. But now she did and I saw a flush of amazement come over her face.

"Judy?"

They were both babbling at once. Imagine! Coincidence! Terrific to see you again! Old friends from New York days, I gathered. (High-school chums? Pals in Greenwich Village?) Lost touch, hadn't seen each other in years. Judy, an aspiring actress, just passing time as a waitress. Sure. Been here five years; still hoping. Must get together some time. Maybe tonight after work? Apartment on Ohio between

Westwood and Federal, practically around the corner from here. Listen, see you in a little while — can't stay and gab. Is the wine okay, sir? Glad to hear it. My God, Dana Greene, imagine that!

Judy poured us our wine and moved along.

Dana couldn't get over it. Imagine — Judy Glass, waiting tables right in the restaurant where we were eating!

My guess was right on both counts: they had gone to high school together in the Bronx, hung out together in the Village afterward. Really close friends: wonderful to rediscover her. Three sips of wine and Dana jumped up and went across the room to talk to her newfound old pal some more. I didn't like that: diversion of interest. Broke the rhythm of mutual seduction. Little did I know. I saw them giggling and whispering and nodding. About what? I would have been amazed. You too. The chitchat went on and on. Old Pierre, the boss, scowled: get on with your work, Mademoiselle. Judy went in back. Dana returned to the table. Said something to Louise that I couldn't hear. Louise grinned. The two of them got up, excused themselves, went toward the bathroom together. Judy was still back there somewhere too. What the hell was brewing? Gone a long time. Louise returned; Dana didn't. I gave her a quizzical look.

Louise said, looking mischievous, "How would you feel if Judy comes home with us tonight, Charlie?"

That startled me. "Instead of Dana?"

"Also."

"Three women?" I was utterly floored. "Jesus Christ."

"Think you can handle it?"

"I could try," I said, still stunned. "God Almighty! *Three!*"

"Dana thought it might be fun. A really Los Angeles thing to do. She can be very impulsive that way."

It took a couple more bathroom conferences for them to work everything out. Somehow they thought it was crass to discuss the logistics in front of me. But finally it was all set up. The restaurant would close around eleven; it would take a little time for the employees to cash out, but Judy could be at my place by half past. A late evening, but worth it, all things considered.

The rest of dinner was an anticlimax. We talked about the weather, the food, the wine, Dana's screenwriting ambitions. But we all had our minds on what was coming up later. Now and then Judy, busy at other tables, shot a glance at me. Second thoughts? I wondered. Or just sizing me up? I shot a few glances at her. I felt dizzy, dazzled, astounded. Would I be equal to the task? A foursome instead of a threesome? A one-man orgy? Sure. God help me, I had to be equal to it. Or else.

We dragged the meal out till half past nine. I drove to my place, Dana and Louise following in Louise's car. Upstairs. Soft music, low lights. Drinks. Kept clothes on while waiting for Judy. Not polite to jump the first two ladies before number three shows up.

Long wait. Eleven-thirty. Quarter to. Judy getting cold feet?

Midnight. Doorbell.

Judy. "I thought we'd never finish up tonight! Hey, what a cool place you have, Charlie!"

"Would you like a drink? A joint?"

"Sure. Sure."

We were all a little nervous. The big moment approaching and nobody quite certain how to start it off.

Things simply started themselves off: a sudden exchange of glances, grins, nods, and into the bedroom we went and the clothes dropped away. And then we were one naked heap on top of the water bed.

So it began, this extraordinary event. The wildest fantasy you could imagine? Sure. But I'm here to tell you that it's possible to get too much of a good thing. Go ahead, laugh.

They certainly were gorgeous. Louise trim and athletic and darkly tanned, Dana pale beneath her clothing and breastier than she seemed when dressed, Judy plump-rumped, red-haired, freckled down to her belly. We were all pretty stoned and piled on each other like demented teen-agers. I got my right hand onto one of Judy's soft, jiggling breasts and my left onto one of Dana's firmer ones and put my tongue into Louise's mouth, and somebody's hand passed between my thighs, and I brought my knee up between some-body else's thighs so she could rub back and forth on it, and then abruptly I was fucking Louise — start with the familiar one, work into it slowly — while trying to find Dana and Judy with my fingers or toes or anything else I didn't happen to be using on Louise.

The perfect deal, you say? Well, maybe. But also a little confusing and distracting. There were all sorts of things to think about. For example I didn't want to get so carried away with Louise that I'd have nothing left for the other two.

Luckily Louise always came easily and quickly, so I was able to bring her to her pleasure without expending a lot of my own energy, and I turned to find one of the others.

But they were busy with each other. Licking and grappling, slurping away merrily. I realized now that they had been better chums back in the old New York days than they had mentioned. It was a turn-on to watch them, sure, but finally I had to slide myself between them to remind them I was here. I peeled them apart and Dana came into my arms and I went into Dana. She was heated up and ready, wild, even, and as her hips began a frantic triple-time pumping I had to catch her and slow her down or she would finish me off in six seconds flat. A little humiliating, really, having to ease her back like that. But for me the first come is always by far the best, and I didn't want this once-in-a-lifetime event to be over so fast. So that was something else distracting to think about. I clung to Dana for as much of the ride as I could take, but finally I had to pull out and finish her by hand, while sliding over into Judy. Louise was moving around in the background somewhere. She was one more thing to worry about, really, because I didn't want to ignore anyone even for a minute, and there wasn't enough of me to go around. I shouldn't have worried all that much. Louise could take care of herself, I knew, and would, and did. But I am a conscientious sort of guy in these matters.

I know, I make it sound like it was a lot of work, and there you are sitting there telling me that you'd have been happy to have taken my place if I found it all that much of a bother. Well, let me tell you, I know there are a lot worse

things to complain about than finding yourself in bed with
too many women at once. But it *was* a lot of work. Really.
A stunt like that has problems as well as rewards. Still and
all, I have to admit it wasn't such a terrible ordeal. Just a
little complicated.

I was in the rhythm of it now — you know how it is, when
you get past that first fear of coming too soon, and feel like
an iron man who can go on forever? — and I swung around
from Judy to Louise again, and back to Dana, and on to
Judy. While I was with Louise, Dana and Judy seemed very
capable of keeping each other occupied. While I was with
either of the other two, Louise improvised with one or another or all three of us at once. It went on and on. I was
swimming in a sea of pussy. Wherever I moved there was a
breast in my hand and one in my mouth and somebody's
thighs wrapped around my middle. Our bodies were shiny
with sweat; we were laughing, gasping, dizzy with the cra-
ziness of it.

Then I knew I would drop dead if it went on one more
minute, and I reached for Louise and entered her and began
to move in the special rhythm that brings on my orgasm.
She knew at once what I was doing: she slipped into a
reciprocating rhythm and whispered little encouraging things
into my ear and I cut loose with the most gigantic come I
am ever going to have.

And rolled off the bed, chuckling to myself, and lay on
the floor in a stupor for I don't know how long while sounds
of ecstasy came from the bed above me. Somewhere in the
night I found enough strength to get back into the fray for

another round or two. But by three in the morning we had all had enough, and then some. I opened the bedroom windows to let the place air out, and one by one we showered and the girls dressed, and we went into the living room, weary and dazed and a little sheepish, all of us stunned by everything that had passed between us this weird night. Dana and Judy left first. Louise lingered for one last joint.

"Well?" she said. "Satisfied now?"

"Am I ever," I said.

What I didn't tell her then, but will confess to you now, is that I wasn't. Not really. Three at once is a remarkable thing. Extraordinary. Unbelievable, almost. But not really satisfying, in terms of my original fantasy. It was too hectic, too mechanical, more work than play. Or so it seems to me, looking back on it now.

Is that hard to believe? Maybe I'm being too picky, I guess. Some guys are never satisfied with anything.

But really: all I wanted was *two*. Not three. Just two. Fucking one, caressing another — switching — switching back — calmly, attentively, sharing my bed with two lovely women, concentrating on them both, fully, without any extraneous distractions. Not an endurance contest or a circus event but a divine adventure in sensuality.

Well, it was never to be, for me. We set it up and then by accident a third woman got involved and I could never set it up again the right way. Louise met a real-estate tycoon a few weeks later and moved to Phoenix. I phoned Dana but she told me she was going back to New York. Le Provence closed and I don't know where Judy went. And the seventies ended and life got a lot more sedate for most of us, especially where stuff like threesomes were concerned. So I still haven't ever been to bed with two women at once, though I once did it with three. Ironic, I guess.

Two at once — I still fantasize about it.

I guess it's not ever going to come to pass. But I live in hope.

CITRE ET TRANS

S a m u e l   R .   D e l a n y

•

"I may be bringing someone home with me," [Turkish] John said. "A man, I mean." John had a long nose. "You won't mind, will you? We'll use the bed in the kitchen; I promise we won't bother you. But . . ." John's blond hair was half gray; his skin was faintly wrinkled and very dry — "it probably isn't a good idea to mention it to DeLys."

"I won't," I said. "I promise. By the time she's back, I'll be gone anyway."

"I meant in a letter, or something. But believe me," he said, "I only pick up nice men. Or boys. There won't be any trouble."

And later, on the cot bed in the front room of the tiny, two-room Anaphiotika house, set in the mountain behind the Acropolis, I went to sleep.

In 'Stamboul, just off Istiqlal, John had had a sumptuous third-floor apartment, full of copper coffee tables, towering plants, rich rugs and hangings. When I'd been staying at the Youth Hostel, one afternoon he'd fed me a wonderful high tea at his place that had kept me going for two days. A pocket full of the leftovers, in a cloth napkin, had — an hour later — even made lunch for towering, timid Jerry.

I woke up to whispered Greek, the lock, and two more Greek voices. One laughed as though he were coughing. *Shhhh*ing them, John herded two sailors, in their whites, through the room. The squat one halted in the door to the kitchen (in which was DeLys's bed that John used), to paw the hanging back. He had a beer bottle in one hand. He laughed hoarsely once more. Then the tall one, towering him by almost two heads, shoved past, with John right after.

I turned over — then turned back. Frowning, I reached down and pulled my wallet out of the pocket of my jeans where I'd dropped them over the neck of my guitar case sticking from under the bed; it was also my suitcase. I sat, slipped the wallet behind the books on the shelf beside me. Then I lay back down.

John came back through the hanging. All he wore now was a blue shirt with yellow flowers. He squatted beside me, knees jackknifed up, to whisper: "There're two of them, I'm afraid. So if you wanted to entertain one — just to keep him busy, while I did the other one — really, I wouldn't mind. Actually, it would be a sort of favor."

"I'm sorry, John," I said. "Thanks. But I'm awfully tired."

"All right." He patted my forearm, where it was bent under my cheek. He smelled drunk. "But you can't say I didn't ask. And I certainly don't mind sharing — if you change your mind." Then he said: "I haven't spoken Demotiki with anyone in more than a year. I'm surprised I'm doing as well as I am." Chuckling, he was up and back into the kitchen, thin buttocks grinding below blue and yellow shirt tails. He disappeared around the hanging, into the lighted kitchen, Greek, and laughter.

I drifted off — despite the noise . . .

Something bumped my arm. I opened my eyes. The little lamp in the corner was on. The squat sailor stood by my bed, leg pressed against my arm. Looking down at me, with one hand he joggled his crotch. Then he said, questioningly: *"Poosty-poosty . . . ?"*

I looked up. "Huh . . . ?"

"Poosty-poosty!" He rubbed with broad, Gypsy dark fingers. A gold ring hugged deep into the middle one's flesh. Pointing at my face with his other hand, he began to thumb open the buttons around his lap-flap. Once he reached over to squeeze my backside. Hard, too.

"Aw, *hey* . . . *!"* I pushed. "No . . . No . . . !" I made dismissive gestures. "I don't want to. *Dthen thello. Phevge! Phevge!"* (I don't want to! Go away! Go away!)

"Ne!" Then he repeated, *"Poosty-poosty,"* emphatically.

The flap fell from black groin hair, that, I swear, went halfway up his belly. His penis swung up, two-thirds the length of mine, half-again as thick. His nails were worn short from labor, and you could tell his palms and the insides of his fingers were rock rough.

"Hey, come on!" I pulled back and tried to sit up. "Cut it out, will you? *Dthen thello na kanome parea!*" (I don't want to mess around with you!)

But he grabbed the back of my head to pull my face at his groin — hard enough to hurt my neck. For a moment, I figured maybe I should go along, so he wouldn't hurt me more. I opened my mouth to take him — and he pushed in, hard. I tasted the bitter sharpness of the cologne he'd doused himself with — and cologne on a dick is my least favorite taste in the world. Under it was the sweat of someone who'd been drinking steadily at least two days. While he clawed into the back of my neck, I thought: This is stupid. I tried to pry my head from under his hand and push him out with my tongue. And thought I'd done it; but he'd just moved, fast — across the bed, on one knee.

It was a hot night. I hadn't been sleeping with any covers.

He grabbed my underpants and, when I tried to dodge away, ripped them down my legs.

"Hey — !" I squirmed around, trying to pull them back up.

But he pushed me, hard, down on the bed. With one knee on my buttock and leaning full on my shoulders, he shouted into the other room — while I managed to lift myself (and him) up first on one elbow, then on the other.

I was about to try and twist him off, so I didn't see the tall one come through; but suddenly he loomed, to grab my

123

arms and yank both, by my wrists, forward. I went off my elbows and down. The sailor on top began to finger between my buttocks. "Ow!" I said. "Ow — stop! . . . *Pauete!*" That made the sailor holding my arms laugh — because it was both formal and plural; and it probably struck him as a funny time for me to be asking him formally to stop.

The tall one let go one wrist and made as if to sock me in the face. He had immense hands. And when he did it, his knuckles looked like they were coming at me hard. I jerked my head aside, squeezed my eyes, and said: "*Ahhh . . . !*"

But nothing connected — it was only a feint. Still, I hit my jaw on the bed's iron rim.

When I opened my eyes, the tall one grinned, and said: "Ha-*Ha!*" — then shook one finger, in a slow warning. Still holding my wrist with one hand, he moved to the right, grabbed my leg just above the knee, and yanked it aside.

The one on top got himself in, then. Holding both my shoulders, he pushed, mumbling in Greek. The tall one moved back to take my free wrist again and squatted there, his face very close. He kind of smiled, curious. His breath smelled like Sen-sen; or maybe chewing gum. He had very black hair (his white cap was still on), hazel eyes, and dark skin. (By his knee, the other's cap had fallen on the rug.) Cajolingly, he began to say, now in Greek, now in English: "You like . . . ! You like . . . ! *Su aresi . . . ! Good boy . . . ! Su aresi . . . !* You like . . . !"

I grunted. "I *don't* like! It *hurts*, you asshole . . . !"

This pharmacologist, who'd first fucked me, told me that if I pushed out as if I was taking a shit, it wouldn't sting.

But not this time.

The one on me bit my shoulder and, panting, came. The one kneeling glanced up at him, then sighed too, let go, stood, and grunted down at me, as if to say, "See, it wasn't that bad. . . ?"

The one behind got off the bed and stood, pushing himself back into his uniform. Once he said to me, in English: "Good! See? You like!" like the tall one had. He picked up his cap from the floor — and (he'd missed two buttons on his lap) pulled it carefully over his head, then pushed one side back up to get the right angle.

I sucked my teeth at him and tried to look disgusted. Frankly, though, I was scared to death.

In Greek the squat one said: *You want him now? I'll hold him for you —*

The tall one said: *You jerk-off! Let's just get out of here!*

The squat one bent down again, picked up my jeans, and began to finger through my pockets. Then the tall one drew back his hand with the same feint he'd used on me: *Come on! Forget that, jerk-off! Let's get out of here, I told you!*

The squat one threw my jeans back down, and they went through the kitchen hanging. There was a back door, but I don't remember if I heard it or not.

I lay on the bed a minute, without moving, propped up on one elbow. Then I reached back between my buttocks. When I looked at my fingers, there were little pads of blood on two fingertips. I got up and went to the stall toilet in the corner —

Urine puddled the stone floor. On DeLys's blue rug, it

had darkened an area three times the size of someone's head.
John must have sent one of them in to use the toilet while
I was still sleeping — before the first guy woke me.

I reached inside, holding the jamb with one hand, and
got some paper from the almost empty roll. Still standing, I
wiped myself, but with a blotting motion. It hurt too much
to rub. When I looked at the yellow paper, there was a red
smear, with some drops running from it, and slimy stuff on
one side. My rectum stung like hell.

I felt like I had to take a crap in the worst way; but the
other thing the pharmacologist had said was to wait at least
half an hour before you did that.

When I went back to the bed, I saw the light in the
kitchen had been turned out. As I sat down, gingerly, on the
edge, on one cheek more than the other, from the dark behind
the hanging, John asked: "Are you all right in there?" He
sounded plaintive. For a moment I wondered if he was tied
up or something.

I called back: "I think so." Then: "Yeah, I'm okay."

A moment later: "Did they take anything from you?"

I pulled my jeans back across the floor toward the bed
with my foot. Then I looked at the book shelf. Between fat
volumes by Mann and Michener was a much read Dell paperback of Vonnegut's *Cat's Cradle*, a quarto hardcover of
Daisy Ashford's *The Young Visitors*, a chapbook of poems by
Joyce Johnson, and Heidi's copy of *L'Ecume de jour*, which
every few hours I'd taken out to struggle through another
paragraph of Vian's playful French.

"No," I said. "My wallet's safe."

At the very end were the paperbacks of my own few novels — and the typewritten sheaf of my wife's poems, sticking up between two of them. Wherever I stayed, I'd always put them on a shelf so I could see them. To make me feel better. They were the books I'd stuck my wallet behind.

"Good," John said. Twenty seconds later, he said: "I don't think they'll come back." And, a few seconds on: "Good-night."

After a minute, I got up again, went to the kitchen door, and switched off the little lamp. I didn't even look behind the hanging. (The big light, still out, you had to stand in the middle of the room to reach up and turn on.) But John wasn't asking for help. So I went back and lay down.

I tried to think of all the reasons I hadn't called for help. They might have beat me up, or hurt me more than they had. What would neighbors — or the police — have thought, coming in and finding me like that? Or thought of John? I might have gotten DeLys in trouble with Costas, from whom she rented the house. Or I might have gotten Costas in trouble with the police: he was a nice guy — a Greek law student at Harvard, home for spring break, who probably wasn't supposd to be renting his house out to foreigners anyway. But, lying there, I couldn't really be sure if any of those thoughts had been in my mind while it had been happening.

Again, I pushed out like I was trying to shit.

The stinging was just as painful. Then a muscle in back of my left thigh cramped sharply enough to make me cry out.

* * *

A good number of people were on the platform when I got there. I had my guitar case — and a shopping bag. At the bottom of the bag was Heidi's Vian. Then my underwear and my balled-up suit. On the top were my novels. Two had actually been published while I was here — though I'd written them before. My wife had sent me a single copy of each, as they came out. I'd figured to reread the newest one on the train — for more typographical mistakes; or for stylistic changes I might want to make. And maybe the typescript of her poems. It was as sunny as it had been on the Piraeus docks when I'd seen Heidi off to Aegina. Shabby-coated lottery vendors ambled about. Ticket streamers tentacled their sticks. A cart rolled by, selling milk-pudding and spinach pie and warm Orangata, big wheels grumbling and squeaking. Sailors and soldiers stood in groups, talking together, among the civilian passengers.

When I saw him — the tall one — with four others in their whites, my heart thudded hard enough to hurt my throat, from the surprise. The back of my neck grew wet. I swallowed a few times — and tried to get my breath back. But — no! — I wasn't going to go up to the other end of the platform. I wasn't going to let the son of a bitch run me all around the train station. I took a deep breath, turned, and looked toward the empty tracks.

But I hoped the train would hurry up.

Not that he could do anything here, with all these people.

128

The third time I glanced at him, he was looking at me — smiling. He was smiling!

Another surge of fear; but it wasn't as big as the terror at my initial recognition.

Next time I caught him looking, I didn't look away.

So he raised his hand — and waved: that little "go away" gesture that, in Greek, means "come over here."

When I frowned, he broke from his group to lope toward me.

He came up with a burst of Greek: *"Kalimera, sas! Ti kanis? Kalla!"* (Hello, you! How you doing? All right?)

"Kalimera," I said, dry as a phrase book.

But with his big (nervous? Probably, but I didn't catch it then) smile, he rattled on. In front of me, the creaseless white of his uniform was as near-blinding as a tombstone at noon; he towered over me by a head and a half. Now, with a scowl, he explained: *". . . Dthen eine philos mou . . . Dthen eini kalos, to peidi . . ."* He isn't a friend of mine . . . he's no good, that fellow . . . Where're you going? It's beautiful today . . . Yes? (*"Orea, simera . . . Ne?"*) You all right? He's crazy, that guy. He just gets everybody in trouble. Me, I don't do things like that. I don't like him. I go out with him, I always get in trouble — like with you and your friend, up there, that night. That wasn't any good. You're taking the train today? Where're you going? You're Negro, aren't you? (*"Mavros, esis?"*) You like it here, in Greece? It's a beautiful country, isn't it? You had a good time? How long have you been here?

I didn't want to tell him where I was going; so I mimed ignorance at half his questions, wondering just what part he thought *he'd* played in the night before last.

I was surprised, though, I wasn't scared any more. At all. Or, really, even that angry. Suddenly, for a demonic joke, I began to ask *him* lots of questions, fast: What was his name? (*"Petros, ego."* Peter, that's me.) Where was he going? (*"Sto 'Saloniki."* To Thessalonika.) Where was he from? (Some little mountain town I'd never heard of before.) Did he like the Navy? (With wavering hand, *"Etsi-getsi."* So-so.) He answered them all quite seriously, the grin gone and — I guess — a slightly bewildered look, hanging above me, in its place.

Finally, though, he dropped a hand on my shoulder and bent to me. He'd come over to me, he explained, because he had something to show me. *No, no — it's all right. Let me show it to you. Here.* He went digging in his back pocket — for a moment I thought he was going to pull out his wallet to show me pictures. But when his hand came back around, he was holding a knife. *No, don't be afraid. Don't be afraid — I just want to show you something.* I pulled back, but, by the shoulder, he forced me forward — still smiling. *Here,* he said. *Here — go on. You take it. Go ahead. Take it. Hold it.* While he held the knife in his amazingly large hand, I saw the nails on his big fingers were clean, evenly clipped, and with ivory scimiters about the crowns — under clear polish.

Like many Greek men, he wore his little nail half an inch or more long.

I hadn't noticed any of that, the night at DeLys's.

I took the closed knife from him and thought: Greek sailors don't usually have manicures. Briefly I wondered if he was queer himself.

He said: *"Orea, eine . . . ?"* (Beautiful, isn't it . . . ?) He didn't make any other gesture to touch it but, with motions of two fingers together and the odd word, told me to open it up. *It isn't very expensive. It's cheap — but it's a pretty knife. Good. Strong. You like it? It's nice, yes? Come on, open it up. A good knife. That button there — you push it up. To open it. Yes. Come on.*

I pushed the button up, and the blade jumped out, a sliver of light, of metal, of sky. *Here!* He laughed. *It's a good knife, yes?*

I nodded — that is, moved my head to the side, the Greek gesture for Yes. *"Ne,"* I said. *"Kallos, to eine."* (Yes. It's a good one.)

He said in Greek: *You want this knife? You like it? Go on, take it. For you. You keep it. You like it, yes? I give it to you. For a present. Maybe you need it, sometimes. It's a good knife.*

"Yati . . . ?" I asked. (Why are you giving this to me?)

You want to kill me now, he said, with sideways nod, then added a chuckle. *Cut something of mine off, I bet. I wouldn't blame you.*

No, I said. I shook my head (or rather, raised it in negation). *"Ochi,"* I told him, *"You take it."* I pressed the button. But it didn't close.

He took it from me now. There was another pressure point you had to thumb to make the blade slip in. With his big, manicured fingers, he thumbed it. *Like that.* The metal flicked into the silver and tortoise shell handle. *You sure? You don't want it?*

I said: *"Ochi — efharisto. Ochi."* (No — Thank you. No.)

He put it in his back pocket again, and regarded me a little strangely, blinking his green-gray eyes in the sun. Then he said: *"Philli, akomi — emis?"* (We're friends, now — us?)

"Okay," I said, in English. "Just forget it."

"Esis. Ego. O-kay!" he repeated. *You. Me.* "O-kay. You like . . . I like . . ." With a flipped finger, he indicated him and me. "Okay. Friend: me, you." He laughed once more, clapped me on the shoulder, then turned to go back to the others. As he walked away, knife and wallet-square were outlined on one white buttock.

I didn't feel like his friend at all.

The other sailors were laughing again — I'm sure about something else.

I watched them, wondering if I could see some effeminacy in any of their movements — queer sailors, camping it up on the station platform. Him . . . maybe. But not the others.

Just once more he caught me looking and grinned again — before the train came.

When we pulled from the station, his group was still talking out on the platform — so he wasn't on my train. I was glad about that.

That night, in my couchette, while we hurled between Switzerland and Italy, in the dark compartment I thought about the two sailors; and when my body told me what I was about to do, I had some troubled minutes, when it was too easy to imagine the armchair psychiatrists, over their morning yogurt and rolls at the white metal tables in front of American Express, explaining to me (in three languages) how, on some level, I had liked it, that — somehow — I must have wanted it.

While I masturbated, I thought about the thick, rough hands of the squat one, but grown now to the size of the tall one's; and the tall one's hazel eyes and smile — but deprived of the Sen-sen scent; and about sucking the squat one's cock, with all its black hair — except that, for the alcoholic-sweat and cologne, I substituted the slight work-salt of a good-humored housepainter I'd had on the first day I'd got to Athens.

Once I tried to use the knife blade, as he held it, full of sky: nothing happened with it.

At all.

But I used my waking up, with the sailor beside me, his leg against my arm, his hand between his legs. I did it first with fear, then with a committed anger, determined to take something from them, to retrieve some pleasure from what, otherwise, had been just painful, just ugly.

But if I hadn't — I realized, once I'd finished, drifting in the rumbling and rocking train — then, alone with it, unable to talk of it, even with John or Heidi, I simply would have found it too bleak. I'd have been defeated by it — and, more, would have remained defeated. That had been the only way to reseize my imagination, let go of the stinging fear, and use what I could of both to heal.

ELLEN, FROM CHICAGO

Pat A. Williams

•

On the dresser was a small photograph of a woman. It was in an old gilded frame, the kind that tarnishes with age, but this one was kept polished to a warm gleam.

The woman was an aviator. I think I would have guessed that even if it hadn't been for her helmet and the upraised goggles. Her eyes seemed to be looking at a vision or at some great expanse, her smile soft but self-assured. A luster seemed to permeate her brown skin. Heroic? Adventurous? I had to smile at those impressions yet I couldn't take my eyes from her picture.

"That's Trina there," Rose's soft voice said.

I jerked my hand back, though I had barely been touching the photograph. Rose Owens smiled.

"She was one of the first colored flyers," Rose said. "Aviatrices they called them. She was the only one from around these parts."

Rose glanced at the picture a time or two while she put the extra blankets on our beds and I could see the fondness in her gaze. "We came up together," she went on. "We were both in the choir at Reverend Clark's church."

She looked about the room to see that all was in order.

Rose didn't look worn with age and there were only a few strands of gray in her hair, but she did look tired. Sixty-one years of living in the South does that to a black woman.

"Everything's fine, Miss Rose," I said.

She nodded but looked around as if there was still something she thought could be done to make her visitors feel more at home.

We heard a footstep in the hallway and Ellen stepped into the room. At the same time a fragrance of honeysuckle came through the screened window on the night wind.

Rose smiled a greeting at Ellen but she came over to the dresser where I stood. "That's the picture they put in the colored paper down at Cane City," Rose said. "I'll have to show you the pictures in the album I keeps."

"Does she still live here?" Ellen asked.

"She was killed in a crash. A car crash. In France," Rose said. The smile had faded from her lips, but it remained in her eyes. "She had the . . . prettiest hands."

She looked at Ellen and me. "Well, I'll let you girls get your rest." She asked us if there was anything else we needed and when we said, "No thank you," she left.

When I had come upon the photograph, I had been looking at the things on the dresser.

It was something I'd taken to doing at the houses we
stayed in. Looking at, examining, touching the keepsakes —
old perfume bottles, saucer ashtrays, jars filled with marbles
and trinkets, photographs. I continued my exploration of this
dresser though I was very aware of Ellen rummaging in her
travel case, of her footsteps around the bed.

I didn't turn around then because I didn't know what to
say to her.

I am not normally tongue-tied with strangers. Every year
I face a new bunch of them from the front of a classroom.
Things had gone along all right with Ellen, too, at first. I
remembered the moment I'd been brought up short.

We were on the drive from Mobile to Lewiston. Kenneth,
Diego, Albert, Ellen, and I. Kenneth and Diego were joking
with Ellen. She sat against the window and the wind lifted
the collar of her loose white blouse. She was answering some
comment of Kenneth's and she said to him, "Well, you know
the finest black women on the planet came from Chicago,
ain't that right?" And her voice was serious but she smiled
and gave a halfway wink to me.

Something, some little cue in that, caught me off guard
so that I couldn't speak just then. Fortunately Diego dove
in with his own comment.

When I looked into the dresser mirror I saw that Ellen
had put on her light-green kimono. It looked cool and soft.

There was a slight frown on her face, not much more
than a deep thoughtfulness, that accentuated her easy-curv-

ing brows and her wide, full mouth. She ran her hand once
across her Afro cut that in sunlight looked for all the world
like jewels shimmered in it.

When she'd got her washcloth and a little bottle of something and left for the bathroom down the hall, I finally turned
away from the dresser.

I came back from my turn in the bath to find her lying
in bed with the sheet tucked about her and her arms folded
behind her head. She watched me as I got ready for bed.

"Ka-ma-li," she enunciated my name softly. I looked at
her and she raised an eyebrow in question. "What does it
mean?" she said.

"It's the name of a protecting spirit," I said.

"What nation does it come from?" she asked.

"It's Mashona. From Zimbabwe," I said. She smiled
slightly, watching me.

"I like the sound," she said quietly and closed her eyes
for a moment. Her long lashes shadowed her cheeks. The
smile still on her face. Then she opened her eyes and caught
me looking at her.

I walked around to the other twin bed and let my short
robe fall — I had only my panties under it — and slid between
the sheets.

"Are you tired?" Ellen asked.

"It's been a long day," I said.

"Good night, Kamali," she said and there was a subtle
amusement in her voice. The lamp was on her side of the
bed and she pulled the cord on it.

I didn't go to sleep, I was too aware of her there.

137

I thought of the talk she'd given in Mobile two days past.

Ellen, Diego, Kenneth, Albert, and I were following the path of the sixties' civil rights workers through the South. We were on a more modern-day crusade; instead of fighting segregation we were lecturing on African history. Kenneth, Albert, and I all taught at the same college. We had scraped together what funding we could and set off at the end of the school year. We were speaking at churches, summer class-rooms, lodges, sometimes in private homes. We stayed in folks' homes because we couldn't afford hotels. In Mobile, we spoke at a lodge hall.

Something drives Ellen when it comes to her beliefs. I would sit next to her as she stood and talked about ancient African civilizations in Zimbabwe and Egypt. I would be very aware of her then, aware of the very faint orange fragrance she wears. When she spoke I could watch her as closely as I wanted.

The light in her dark eyes burned when she made a point that she wanted her audience not just to know but to believe. Moisture formed on her neck and her brow, and when she became excited a little hoarseness came out in her voice.

I heard her breathing in the bed next to mine, and finally I slept too.

In the morning I woke to find her sitting on the side of her bed. I didn't think that she noticed me watching her right away. She leaned forward, examining her hands. All of the passion that could fill her face seemed to be gone; only a faint smile played on her lips.

"Good morning," she said, without looking up, then a moment later she did, and smiled. Caught again. I smiled back at her. "What were you thinking about?" I said.

"How quick the time passes," she said. "How few people we'll reach this summer after all. But," she said, shrugging, "I'm thankful for even small favors."

"I don't see how anyone could listen to you and not believe every word you say," I said.

There was a mischievous spark in her eye. "Thank you."

We held each other's gaze for a long time. Morning sounds came from the window and downstairs — some farm machinery droning across the fields, jaybirds hijinking out in the woods, voices in the kitchen. I think it was just then that something was decided between us. "What are you thinking about?" she said.

"You."

I lay on my stomach and the pressure against my mons felt good. My fingers pushed into the pillow. There was no mischief in her eyes now, no amusement on her face. It was open.

"Miss Rose's friend," I said, "was not from Chicago. But she sure was fine."

Ellen smiled. Uh oh, now who was shy? She bit her bottom lip just a little.

I got out of bed and put on my robe — for some reason — and I fastened it loosely. The beds were right beside each other so all I needed to do was reach out to stroke her cheek. For a moment I allowed my hand to lie on the soft, soft skin

139

of her shoulder beneath her kimono. I imagined how her breast would feel, imagined the taste of her plum brown nipple. I was aware of her close, fresh, morning smell.

"Lady," one of us said.

I sat down beside her. "This is a long trip," I said. "And I find you very attractive."

She placed a hand on my thigh where my robe fell open and rubbed me gently. We kissed as softly as her touch.

We held each other breast to breast and played just a moment with the tips of our tongues on our lips, inside our mouths. She moaned and just then there was a sudden sound from the dresser. A loud click. We both jumped.

No one was there, but the picture of Trina had fallen over. Ellen chuckled.

"Yes ma'am, Miss Trina."

A moment later we heard footsteps in the hallway.

Miss Rose set a cup of strawberries and two glasses of cold milk in a place she cleared on the dresser. She inquired as to how we had slept and I wondered if she noticed the odor that our touching had brought.

Rose carefully set Trina's picture upright again. "Once Trina took me up in that airplane." Rose carefully raised her hand from the picture. "I was so scared. But I wasn't worried. Ain't that funny? I wouldn'a gone up with nobody else but Trina."

She looked at us and I saw, for the first time, how sharp and young her eyes were.

"This was her second home too. She was always over here. Little place where she grew up, they turned into a colored library. I have to show you my picture album before you go."

Ellen still sat on the bed but I gathered my things to go to the bathroom. I wanted to be alone for just a little time. I wanted a quiet place for my thoughts of what was happening.

Once there, I stood in front of the mirror and pushed my long dreadlocks back so that they lay across my shoulders. Kenneth called them my lion locks. I touched my face, taking account of the golden-brown skin, the cheekbones and brown eyes and assuring myself that Ellen liked them.

The fellows were downstairs. They commented on how refreshed we looked that morning. Kenneth looked at us closely — he knew something, I'm sure — and he said, "You two complement each other."

We sat next to one another, and all through breakfast my leg lay next to, barely touching, hers.

Toward the end of breakfast Rose held court. She told us the history of her house, built for the white Owens by her great-grandparents when they were still slaves. Now the black Owens lived in it.

Rachel, who ran the beauty parlor in the basement, came up to join us. She was light-skinned with gray eyes and a blond streak in her hair. She grinned as she sat back, crossed her legs, and said, "Miss Rose don't know it, but she's the state historian."

The morning lingered full of sounds and smells that I recalled from growing up in that part of the country. The morning radio gospel show from Memphis, the smell of dry

141

grass and dust. It was already hot, and there were beads of sweat on the back of Ellen's hand.

The day grew warmer; the wind died, and touching the bright chrome on a car sitting in the sun could burn you.

We would give another talk that night, so we were staying the day. I lay across the bed in our room that afternoon, attempting to keep cool. The curtains were drawn against the heat so the light was dim. The door opened and Ellen came in.

She thought that I was sleeping because she moved quietly across the room to her satchel. I watched her take out a small book and pick up her straw sun hat from the chair. "Ellen," I said.

She looked toward my bed and then walked over. "Baby, I didn't mean to wake you," she said.

When she sat down I reached up and touched her hair, warm from the sun. My fingers ran easily down her back. She shivered a little. "You're not going to let up are you?" she said.

"No."

She chuckled. "All right."

Then she whispered, "Nobody's objecting to the way this is going anyway."

I touched my finger to her lips and she kissed it. And my hand rubbed across her breast when I lowered it. It rested on her thigh. And caressed her hip.

"Kamali, Kamali," she whispered, leaning over me. I pulled her body to me. My hand on her hip stroked firmer, moving up the fabric of her skirt. When I am about to touch another woman, when I'm just beginning to, I can already taste her, her sweat and her juices and I can already feel my fingers in her wet places. Ellen had filled my mouth already and I swallowed. "Baby," she said and she kissed me.

My hand smoothed around to the damp inside of her thigh. "Come with me," she said, and I nodded. She laughed and pulled back a bit more. "No, come with me to the library. It's closed today. But Miss Rose gave me a key. She said I could spend the afternoon there. I'm going to give them my copy of *Stolen Legacy*."

We walked to the library, wide sun hats on our heads, holding hands because I didn't want to lose contact with her flesh. I listened to the sound of her voice as much as to her words when she spoke of her passion, the ancients. There were ancient black civilizations, people had to know that. Philosophies we had founded at the beginnings of time were still around today.

Lies had covered all of that but we were going to uncover the truths. People had to know. *Had to.* I nodded my agreement. Her passion had drawn me to her long before I knew her body.

It was cool — almost — inside the tiny one-room library.

The Trina Brown Library. We could hear the waters of a stream that passed a few feet away, shaded by the same gigantic oaks that covered the tiny building. We walked about, fingers linked, and looked at the precious old volumes.

"Miss Rose takes care of this place," Ellen said. "She brings flowers once a week. In the winter she gets them from the florist in town."

Petunias and bachelor's buttons sat in a blue vase by a window. There was a couch there, worn and old and soft. Ellen pulled me to her. I wrapped my arms around her, her breasts pressed against mine; her whole body against mine thrilled me.

We kissed long and slowly, tasting and sucking each other. I pressed into Ellen and she moaned.

I smoothed her body with my hands and she caressed me, kneading me all the way down my back, my behind. I opened the front of her dress, slowly. When we were both naked we lay down on the couch. I was wet, my clit was hard, and when her hand brushed between my legs it sent tremors through me.

She pulled me down onto her. "Is it going to be good?" she whispered and kissed me again before I could answer.

Her nipples hardened between my fingers as I pulled and squeezed them. I moved slowly between her legs. Kissing her neck and down to her shoulders. Such a fine, pretty woman, such a sweet, good-tasting thing.

I remembered the sweat on her neck, I remembered her wink and the first time her leg touched mine in the backseat of the car. Fine, pretty Chicago woman. She found my mouth again, kissed me hard.

I bit softly at her nipples, slowly licked the sweat salt on her stomach, then found the juices between her legs and drank them. I licked the little bud there and heard the breath rushing in her and her moaning. I felt her hands all in my locks and when she pulled me up and kissed me roughly, clawing at my back, I loved it.

She rode me, her mons pushing deeper into mine, pressing harder as it built up in me and I wanted to pee and I wanted to come. I shook and held her close enough to be a part of me.

I held her as her trembling eased and as I caught my breath. Her hands were already exploring my body again. She moved into me, feeling my wetness as she sucked my breasts, ran her tongue into my navel. . . .

I opened again, wide.

We went down to the stream sometime afterward and climbed in naked. The water was the coolest and sweetest.

Then we walked across the soft grass back to the library.

Ellen ran her finger down the spine of the slim little book — her favorite — that she was leaving behind; she took my hand again and we left. We joked that we should have exchanged dresses and seen if anyone would notice.

"You girls have a nice afternoon?" Rose said. She did not look up from the cake that she was decorating with berries and peach slices.

Ellen pressed her lips into a smile, her dimple showing.

I put on some raspberry tea — hot things in hot weather cool you down, so they say — and called down to Rachel and her customer to come up and join us.

Rose did show us her picture album.

Late that night after our talk, Rachel called us into her beauty shop where she had Rose on the recliner chair giving her a foot rub.

Rose had the album on her lap. "Come over here and see this," she said to us.

145

There was a picture of Trina in the plane that she flew down from Cincinnati. There was Trina and Rose in their choir robes in front of the church. Here was Trina and Rose caught by somebody's camera while they lay sleeping under a shade tree. Here was Trina Brown in her fine fur coat and her scarf and her genuine Spanish leather boots getting ready to leave for overseas.

"Kind of fond of that flyer, wasn't you, Rose?" Rachel smiled.

Rose looked down into her photograph album. "She's my hist'ry."

THE GOLDEN BOY:
Adventures in
Memory Adjustment

Carol A. Queen

•

When I met Jon he was just past chubby, melted down into a lithe boy who was starting to show signs of man. He was a young man the way a colt is part gangly animal and part magical apparition. He wore his awkwardness like a beetle wears its shell, to cover up the soft inside.

He was my high school friend. He sometimes flirted with me, just to practice. I watched him hesitating on the cusp of growing up. If he had been more self-assured I would have been smitten, and if I had been any more self-assured I'd have taken him — easy, the way his hormones were trembling and threatening to spill over, like water from a glass. But I was not the one he chose for his first affair.

Mr. White had just been hired to teach at the high school. He was on a three-year contract, and that was all the longer he would stay, because teachers like him are never hired back. He must have interviewed in his one regular suit — he'd never have gotten the job dressed the way he usually did, in old, old clothes, antique three-piece suits and wire-rimmed glasses and a watch and chain. He was hired to teach drama, of course — that's probably why they let him slip by — and English. He *looked* English, actually, like a headmaster at a shabby third cousin of Eton. He had bright, lavishly lashed eyes and a moustache that curled. No one in our remote little town had ever seen anything like him. He was like a time traveler who had taken a very wrong stop. He could not have been expected to have anything in common with a bunch of ranchers' sons and daughters. Nevertheless a few of us had determined that we were not going to be hicks. We were over him like flies on honey.

Jon was skittish around Mr. White from the start, manic even. For about a week he joined the other boys, and raved about what a fruit and a faggot the new teacher was. But by the end of the second week of school he had arranged to join three extracurricular clubs — the Thespians, the school paper, and a modern novel study group — so he could be near him.

On any given day Jon could be found before class, after class, and often at lunch in Mr. White's room. I knew that because I was in the habit of dropping by at those times myself. Of all the students who clustered around the new teacher, I was the closest to understanding just why he seemed so odd. He was so completely different from any other man I'd ever known, in his eccentricity so sweet and strange, that of course I began cruising him almost right away. I was just learning that having sex with a person could teach me things about them and about myself, and I was sure Mr. White was a wealth of things I wanted to know.

But he made no response to my attempts to interest him. Not a negative response — just *none*. He didn't even seem to notice. He took flirtation as another indication of friendliness, and was friendly in return. I didn't feel rejected, exactly, because it dawned on me that Mr. White would never want me the way he wanted Jon.

I watched Jon become a golden boy as the teacher gentled him like a wild thing. He went from edgy and defensive to a secure position as Mr. White's sidekick. He starred in the plays; he was the ace reporter; he grew handsomer and more confident as he was courted.

Our town was so small and so remote that no one saw it for what it was, not even, at first, Jon himself. Everybody thought they knew what a faggot was — it was practically synonymous with "stranger" — but after they got to know Mr. White he turned out not to fit the ideas they had, and the fag-baiting ceased and was forgotten. Only I knew that a careful dance was being done between Jon and Mr. White — I knew it because I had wanted to do that dance myself. I was their witness first in secret, and later I was the only one either of them trusted to talk about the other. So in the end I danced with them, a sometimes-awkward third, as Jon grew more golden and Mr. White grew hungry for him.

◦ ◦ ◦

It was late in our senior year. One night after a play rehearsal ended early we got in Mr. White's old round Volvo and drove to his house. Neither Jon nor I was expected home for a couple of hours, and it was not the first time the three of us had stolen time so we could hang out together away from school. Mr. White had no friends in town except those few pet students who weren't put off by his eccentricity, and Jon and I liked to escape our student roles and pretend we were grownups who could spend our time as we liked. Besides, befriending Mr. White had made us feel less like we belonged in our community, and all year long we'd spent as much time with him as we could — a support system had formed between the three of us to the exclusion of everyone else.

There was a massage table set up in the living room, although I was sure it was hardly ever used. As far as I knew Mr. White rarely had guests of any kind. But when Jon saw it he insisted that he wanted a massage; he'd never had a real one, he wanted to try it.

"I can't do it through clothes," Mr. White said, and I really think he was trying to put Jon off. But Jon replied, "I'll take them off, then," and began shucking his t-shirt. For a split second the man looked panicked, but when he glanced over at me, for help or permission, I held out a joint I had fished from my bag. I had a feeling I was supposed to be there for this, that maybe Jon wouldn't have been so forward

if he and the teacher had been alone. "Go ahead, I'm occupied," I said, pulling a couple of Mr. White's art books
off the shelf, opening *The Collected Aubrey Beardsley.* I didn't
look at it, though. I watched Jon's body emerge, watched
the golden hairs on his arms and legs catch the low lamplight.
And I watched Mr. White's eyes follow his movements; Jon
was turned away so he couldn't see how both of us lapped
up his beauty as he revealed it. He was slender, just beginning
to muscle, and his skin looked so soft that I wondered how
Mr. White would be able to touch it. My panties felt slick.
I squeezed my legs together and watched as Jon got on the
table. All nonchalance, he lay back with his head on his hands
like a boy in an Eakins painting, like it was a century ago
and he'd just crawled out of the swimming hole to lie in the
sun, his cock lolling on his thigh, but I saw him trying to
control his too-fast breath, I saw he had put his hands behind
his head to hide their shaking.

"I feel funny being the only one naked," he said, and he
wasn't addressing this to me. Mr. White's eyes went wide,
he pretended not to hear as he hunted in a heavy old cabinet
for massage oil, but Jon insisted: "Take your clothes off too.
I feel silly like this."

I tried to disappear into the cushions. I was afraid Mr.
White wouldn't do anything with me there; I wanted to watch
his hands caressing Jon, and I wanted to see *him* naked, too.
More, I wanted something to happen to give Mr. White
pleasure — I thought about how lonely he must be, his bed
as empty as his massage table. He desired Jon, and I wanted

him to have him. I hid behind the big volume of Beardsley, lowering my eyes in intent study of the few young dandies sprouting huge cocks, and watched my two friends through my lowered lashes.

For twenty years I have marveled at Mr. White's courage in the face of the fear he must have felt: stripping his clothes off in front of a woman (I don't think he ever had), exposing his body so like the naked androgynes in the Maxfield Parrish prints that decorated his walls, and reaching to touch a boy who, by the laws of the state was only just barely old enough. That night I marveled at the way he looked, even naked, like he had landed in the wrong time, and how looking at them filled me, choked me with lust, and the excitement simmered in me without boiling, for I was only there to witness. The man warmed a pool of oil in his fine, slender hands and touched the boy, just lightly. "Here, turn over," he said.

Jon lay on his stomach on the table, head turned toward me, eyes half-closed. Mr. White held his shoulders for an instant and Jon sighed, giving up a bit of his fright to the warmth of the man's hands on his skin. Then Mr. White began sweeping strokes down Jon's body and I realized I didn't have to pretend not to be there, nor to see: my presence had not prevented their touching, it wouldn't stop now that it had begun. I let the book fall and watched openly, watched Mr. White's cock rise, growing with each stroke as if hands were stroking it to fullness. I watched him grow mesmerized, his hands on the young body he had wanted for so long. I learned how to watch that night, for I could feel the strokes of his oiled hands on me as I watched as if they were on my own flesh, and I could feel Jon's tender boy-skin under my hands as if I were the one touching him. I stayed curled in the corner of the sofa, wanting to be just there, one hand on my pussy squeezing tight and the other holding my breast, realizing that I could make love with both of them just with my eyes.

Mr. White was making love with his hands, and Jon was moving his body subtly into them, responding to the touch in a way I knew was sexual — it was the way I moved when someone touched me. He let out an occasional little sound, and his breath was even now, but beginning to quicken again, not in fear this time. No one has ever touched him like this before, I thought, and another jolt of arousal coursed through me, thinking that Jon was a virgin. The man was exploring him, every inch of skin oiled now and gleaming in the light, every muscle traced and kneaded, every curve of his body voluptuously stroked. Each time he stroked up Jon's thighs and over the muscles of his ass, Mr. White brought his hands closer together, testing the boy's response as he came nearer the cleft of his asscheeks. I could feel my cunt frankly wet through my panties now, and Jon squirmed in an encouraging way each time the hands neared, raising his ass for more pressure. Mr. White responded by stroking harder, pulling the cheeks apart each time; I couldn't see the puckered anal ring from where I was sitting, but I felt sure that if I could, I would come. I wondered if Jon had ever had anything in his ass — when I masturbated I sometimes slid a finger in mine, or fucked myself with a candle, and I thought about him sliding a slick wax taper up his ass in the secrecy of his room, getting used to the feeling and pumping it in and out, and I thought of him fucking himself in the ass and thinking of Mr. White's long, slim cock sliding up into his soft hotness there — and I did come.

I didn't make much noise, but enough for them to hear me. Jon let out a real moan then, and I saw that he had begun to thrust, stroking his cock against the table. Mr. White stopped him with the pressure of a hand. "Turn back over now, Jon," he said, in a voice I had never heard him use, low and sexual and almost enough to make me come a second time.

Jon's cock was hugely hard, an incongruous man's cock jutting up from his boy's body, and seeing it I wanted to climb onto the table and lower myself down on it, take him, be the first, almost as much as I wanted to watch.

I could scarcely believe Mr. White had the self-control not to reach right for it, but he teased Jon — or maybe he was intent on giving him a good massage in spite of himself. He stroked up and down the boy's body, missing the cock each time, but attentive instead to nipples and belly, until Jon started to buck again with desire. A beaded strand of pre-come gleamed in his downy belly-hair like a spider's dewed web, and I wanted to lick it off, but thought if I waited maybe I'd get to watch Mr. White do it.

During the next near-brush with his cock Jon lifted his hand, and for a moment I thought he was going to touch himself in frustration. But he reached for Mr. White and took the man's cock, which leaped and strained at his first tentative touch, and began to stroke it. Mr. White gasped, then said, "Jon . . ." Jon tugged on Mr. White's cock, pulling the man closer. "Your mouth — please . . ." Jon said. "Your mouth, I want it . . . I want to feel it . . ."

Mr. White moved closer, all semblance of massage gone with the boy's request, and stroked Jon's cock a few times, taking its measure, getting the full feel of it in his hands. Then he bent to run his tongue up and down his length — Jon started gasping immediately — and then sucked the head into his mouth. I thought Jon would come right away, but the man knew what he was doing. He remained still until the boy's orgasm ebbed, and then began sucking his cock in earnest, pulling it all the way down his throat, drawing back to just tongue the tip, keeping the rhythm just uneven enough that Jon could keep from coming. He held the boy's balls clasped in one hand and squeezed them — whenever he squeezed them harder I heard Jon gasp.

I had pulled my panties aside and had three fingers deep in my cunt. I was dreaming about kneeling next to Mr. White and taking his cock deep down my throat, maybe wetting a finger and sliding it up his ass, but I was afraid. I was sure he had had his cock sucked by plenty of men. I hadn't done it very much, and didn't want to do it badly by comparison. I contented myself with watching him, trying to figure out what exactly he was doing to Jon. Whatever it was, he was responding like it was an angel whose lips were wrapped around his dick, not just his teacher's.

Jon had begun to murmur: "I want it, I want it . . ." rhythmically, entranced. He was twisting his torso, trying to reach Mr. White's cock with his mouth, trying to suck him in return. Mr. White finally knelt over him on the table, obliging him, and Jon went for his cock with the hunger of an overripe virgin. He held the man by the waist and tried to bring him down closer, tried to get more of his cock, and Mr. White swallowed all of Jon's cock and, with a moan, began thrusting into Jon's mouth. Jon took it, moaning too. His oiled body still gleamed in the lamplight, golden, and he fucked up into his teacher's throat.

I had been coming for five minutes by the time they finally came, Jon shooting with a last hard thrust and what would have been a yell if his mouth hadn't been so full, and Mr. White with a long groan, in immediate response. The boy took the man's come like he'd sucked cock before, but I don't think he ever had. He lay whimpering a little after his blast, suckling at the man's softening cock and breathing hard. After a while Mr. White turned around and held him, and Jon buried his head in his neck and hugged him close — once again I saw the young boy in him, and wondered what would happen now that boy was playing tug-o-war with man.

Mr. White came to me and kissed me, once, lingeringly, before he took Jon into the shower to scrub off the oil, letting me have the scent of the boy's sweet cum. I rose and went to the empty massage table, running my fingertips on the warm oily surface. At my feet the Beardsley book lay open, a black-haired young fop sprouting an enormous erection, fondled by a man much older than he.

Author's Note: Much love and gratitude to the people whose composites make up these portraits — and much love and luck to anyone growing up queer in a small town.

I HAVE SOMETHING FOR YOU

Blake C. Aarens

·

I hadn't planned to wear the double dildo to the Valentine's Day Dance. It was just that I got so turned on wearing it inside my jeans earlier that day. Standing at the mirror, I liked the way I looked and I liked the way I felt. But I wasn't so sure Beverly would share my enthusiasm. She constantly complained about the "outrageous baby dykes" like myself. She was 39 to my 23.

"All right," I'd said to the contrived bulge in my jeans, "I'll introduce you to Beverly next weekend, I promise."

We'd been looking forward to tonight for almost a year, having gotten together six weeks after last year's Lesbian Love Dance. I'd reserved my rental tux over a month ago, and she'd been sewing herself a red silk dress, a project she absolutely refused to let me see beforehand. I didn't want

158

anything to ruin our evening, but I didn't want to sell it short either.

Now, standing in my living room, I undid the buttons on my 501s and slid them down to my ankles; my panties followed suit. I was scheduled to pick Beverly up in 45 minutes. With both hands, I grabbed the end of the jet black dildo that was protruding from my chocolate brown body. Slowly I pulled on it, my hips rolling forward and then pulling back as the tip left my cunt with a wet, sucking sound. I shuddered.

"Go get in the shower," I said in a weak voice. With my pants down around my ankles, I waddled into the bathroom.

I pulled up in front of Beverly's house two minutes ahead of schedule and retrieved my tuxedo jacket from the back seat where I'd draped it to keep the tails from getting crushed. Cradling a dozen roses in my left arm, eleven of them long-stemmed and wrapped in tissue paper, the twelfth fashioned into a wrist corsage, I walked up the front steps. If I knew anything at all about Beverly Carter, M.D., her dress would either be low cut or completely off the shoulder, with little room to even pin a petal, much less a whole flower.

I rang the doorbell and tried to blow my sweaty palms dry. Beverly opened the door, and I lost my voice at the sight of her. She was loveliness itself: her short natural hair glistening, the few strands of gray soft around her face, her breasts practically spilling out of the top of her dress which was, as I'd predicted, off the shoulder. It was also very short. She wore a crinoline underneath which lifted the full skirt away from her round, brown body. Her ample thighs were encased in black hose. My palms were sweating again.

"You like?" Beverly asked, smiling, her mouth as red and moist as the cherries you get with *piña coladas*. I wanted to bite into it. Instead I nodded eagerly and gave her a peck on the cheek and an A-frame hug that kept my pelvis well away from hers. She looked at me puzzled, but I handed her the roses before she could say anything.

We made one hell of an entrance at the dance, classic butch and femme. Several people told us they'd thought we were the other way around. We switched up not just to keep people guessing, but to keep each other interested.

We drank and talked and the d.j., a wild woman in red satin pajamas, the top of which she hadn't bothered to button, kept us jamming on the dance floor.

Every so often Beverly would spin away from me and her dress would rise up as she twirled. I could see the tops of her stockings and the garters that held them up. She watched me watching her.

"You like?" she asked again, coming close to whisper in my ear.

"Yes. I like."

She threw her head back like she does when she comes and laughed out loud. Then she twirled away and danced with her back to me. That meant I could look at her body without having to contend with the demands of her eyes. And I did just that, thinking all the while of what I'd like to do. Liberate her breasts from inside that dress. Run my face along her stockinged legs. Suck on that cherry red mouth. Share my new toy with her.

Why didn't I?

Because I was afraid. Afraid she'd be disgusted at the notion of dykes with dildos. Afraid she'd give me a lecture on the political incorrectness of lesbians using anything remotely resembling a penis during sex. Or worst of all, afraid she'd accuse me of wanting to be a man; or wanting her to be.

But what I really wanted to do was to take her hand and say, Dr. Beverly? Do you realize that I'm wearing half a double dildo inside my body, and the other half I'm saving for you?

"What's the matter?" she asked me, interrupting my thoughts with a touch on the cheek and a worried look on her face.

"Nothing," I said.

The d.j. picked that moment to play the first slow song of the evening. I panicked, dropped Beverly's hand and headed for the table we'd claimed when we first entered the hall.

"What is the matter with you," she said, standing in front of the table with her hands on her hips. "Don't you want to dance with me?"

"Of course I do, just not to this song." I caught myself with my hands crossed over my lap and I forced them to rest lightly on the tabletop.

"To what song, then?"

"I just don't feel like slow dancing."

"It's Valentine's Day," Beverly said, in clipped tones. "That's what it's for."

Just then, my ex-lover, heretofore known only as the "wicked bitch of the West" came up to the table. Her jeri curl was dripping onto her collar. Ignoring me, she held her hand out to Beverly. "You look marvelous. Would you like to dance?"

Looking directly into my eyes, Beverly responded, "I'd love to." She disappeared onto the dance floor.

I gave myself a good talking to. "Look," I said, "you have one of two choices: either go into the bathroom and take that damn thing out of your pants, or go onto the dance floor as you are and show the woman you love what you really got her for Valentine's Day."

"Excuse me," I said, tapping my ex on the shoulder, "but you're dancing with my woman." My ex departed coolly.

I took a deep breath, wrapped my arms around Beverly, and pulled her to me. I felt her body tense up as our thighs met. Then she started moving to the music.

"Oooh. You're bad," she whispered into my ear.

"I try to be."

"Is this for me?"

"It's for both of us, a new friend."

"And just when did you plan to introduce me," Beverly asked, leaning her shoulders away to look into my face.

"I don't know. After the dance. I didn't think I could get up the courage to do it before then."

"Baby," Beverly stopped moving to the music, "as far as

I'm concerned, the dance is over." She took me by the hand and led me off the dance floor. Breezing past the table with me in tow, she picked up her wrap and purse. Out in the parking lot, she pressed me up against the car, kissed me full on the mouth, dropped her keys into my hand and said, "Take me home and fuck me."

I didn't have to be told twice.

I couldn't look at her the whole drive home. I was afraid I'd wreck the car if I did. When I pulled into her driveway and took the key out of the ignition, she was all over me: her mouth on mine, her hands on my breasts, squeezing my nipples through the fabric of my shirt. She started undoing the buttons.

"I'm going to freeze if you undress me out here," I said.

"So come inside." She jumped out of the car and ran giggling into the house.

I followed a trail of clothes to her bedroom. First the wrap, then her shoes, then the red dress. I picked it up off the floor; it was still warm. It smelled like her. When I appeared in the doorway holding it, she laughed.

"Why hold the dress when you can hold the woman?" Sitting on the bed, she was wearing only a merry widow, her skin showing through the white lace. Her stockinged legs were crossed. She motioned for me to come in.

I dropped the dress and went to her. She made me stand perfectly still while she slowly undressed me. First the jacket which she carefully hung over the chair at the foot of her bed. Then the cuff links and buttons which she laid in a neat pile on her dresser. She took my shirt off; I wasn't wearing a bra. She kissed me. My mouth. My throat. The points of both shoulders. My nipples. I lifted my feet out of the shoes; she slid my pants and panties down my legs and off. She grabbed my ass and pulled me to her, ground her thighs into mine until the dildo was smashed between us.

"You are so bad," she said again. I nodded in agreement as she undid the harness that had held the dildo in place. She grabbed the end that was sticking out of my body and began to pull on it. I closed my eyes and groaned. She stopped pulling.

"Oh no," she said, "you have to look at me."

With effort, I opened my eyes, matched her gaze. Slowly, she drew the dildo out of my body, then just as slowly put it back where it had come from. I couldn't control the shaking in my legs.

Beverly bent her knees and teased herself with the free end of the dildo, letting it poke between her legs or just enter her cunt before she'd pull away.

"Work it Dr. Beverly, work it."

"I intend to."

Then she whispered my name and let the dildo enter her a little more. "Alice." More. "Sweet Alice." Finally, we were belly to belly. She clenched her pubic muscles and made the dildo jerk inside me. I sucked in air through clenched teeth. She parted my teeth with her tongue and kissed me.

"Happy Valentine's Day, baby," she said.

BELONGING

Pat Califia

·

"Bartender!" Jerry shouted, loud enough to be heard over the raucous country music and the buzz of a very drunk Saturday-night crowd. He was a handsome kid, but spoiled-looking. In his mid-twenties, he still wore the brooding expression of an adolescent who perpetually feels fucked over and misunderstood. His clothes were cheap synthetics, too flashy for what they had cost him, and they made him seem oddly sleazy for somebody so young: James Dean playing the part of a bookie or a gigolo. He slammed his glass on the counter, not once, but three times, and the startled, portly man at the sink in the middle of the bar hurried over to him, wiping his hands on his apron.

The barkeep was too harassed to notice the details of his obnoxious customer's personal appearance. His tastes ran to plump redheads with balconylike bosoms. But there was somebody else in the bar whose preferred sexual quarry was young men whose expectations far exceeded their willingness to exert themselves. He had tracked Jerry to this noisy lair, and he was enjoying the opportunity to observe that sulky mouth and to laugh silently to himself about the rude and ridiculous things that inevitably came out of it. Much better for a mouth like that to be taught silence. Hidden within the sozzled crowd, this hunter stroked the tool he used to gag his attractive-but-lazy prey. It was in good working order.

"Yeah?" the bartender said, none too friendly. The loudmouth was bobbing and weaving, scowling at the mirror behind the bar, obviously close to losing it.

That bitch Caroline, Jerry thought, the fucking bitch. She won't let me in, and she won't answer my phone calls. How can I get to her? If I could *talk* to her I'd make her understand. It's that guy I saw at her place, I know it, it's *him*, I'll bet he's with her right now and they're screwing their brains out. Shit! What makes her think she can do this to me, the whore? "Scotch and soda," he blared. "On the double."

"Forget it! The only thing I'm serving you is a cup of coffee. Finish what you got and go home."

There was no arguing with that grim, jowly face. Jerry picked up what was left of his drink and jostled his way through the crowd to the other side of the bar. There was a place by the pinball machine where he could lean against the wall. It took him two tries to light a cigarette. "Fuck, I must be high," he thought and tried to focus his eyes on the tip of his nose. Ouch. Yes. I am definitely getting drunk in this here shitkickers' bar. He'd met Caroline in a much classier joint than this.

I must have looked like a fool, he thought, barging around, describing that cunt to everybody. Took me forever to figure out she'd stood me up. Then this woman said, "Be quiet. Sit down and help me finish this champagne." Caroline never said "please" or "thank you" or asked a question, she just told you what to do and you did it, but he couldn't say she was rude, just very sure of herself. *Way* too sure of herself. She was wearing a severely tailored, dark wool suit, and he would have sworn she was wearing a man's shirt and tie if not for the pearly stickpin that held the length of silk in place. Her short, black hair was expensively styled. He remembered thinking, I sure got lucky, this one's old enough to know what women want and rich enough to pay the price.

Drunk as he was, it finally occurred to him that one of the men over by the pool table was not part of the quiet, businesslike game — a handsome bastard with a big, hooked nose and a black beard that made him look grim as hell. He wasn't dressed very nice for a weekend, just faded jeans and a T-shirt, one of those wide garrison belts that cops wear, and a black leather jacket. His hands were so big, you could hardly see the beer can he gripped.

Jerry's bitter reverie recovered from this brief interruption, and flowed on, well rehearsed. All I did was drop by one Friday night. Is that a crime, huh? If a guy's been making it pretty regular with a broad for a couple of weeks, you figure he can drop by without getting arrested, right? Especially if he brings something along, I mean it isn't like I went over there empty-handed, for Chrissake, I *had* a six-pack.

The guy by the pool table turned toward him, hooked his thumb far back between his legs and scratched his balls. He had a contemptuous look on his face, a look that said, "Kiss my ass."

When I rang her bell she didn't even use the intercom to ask who it was, just hit the buzzer and let me in. The front door to her loft wasn't locked. I walked right into her living room. And there's this dude stretched out in the armchair, watching porno movies on the color TV! Boy, was I mad. Anybody else would have slugged her.

Now the big man crossed his arms on his chest and pushed his hips forward a little. By some accident or some genius of self-arrangement, the length of his cock was a visible tube down the inner seam of one leg of his jeans. Then he made it jump. Jerry began to lose the thread of his aggrieved monologue. His mouth was awfully dry. He took a sip from his glass and adjusted the waistband of his slacks. It had been a long time since he'd gotten any. Weeks.

Ever since she'd thrown him out, in fact. She had wheeled around, white-faced, and said, "You were not asked to be here." Step by step she had backed him into the foyer, not seeming to hear him as he demanded angrily who that man was, what was going on, until finally he shouted, "Goddamn-it, I need to know that you belong to me!"

Her face broke into the biggest smile. "Don't worry," she said softly. "I know exactly what you need. And I'm going to make sure you get it." Beguiled by that sweet face and the sweeter promise, he had let her put him out and gone his way, confused but expecting to hear from her any day, to collect his reward for being so patient and understanding.

"Instead, all I get is a goddamn runaround," he told his warm, flat drink.

Thumbs hooked in his pockets, the dark man stroked himself discreetly, fingertips fanning out on his buttoned fly. His eyes flicked toward the back of the bar, then back to Jerry, with a questioning (but still hostile) stare. Here was a promise of satisfaction that would not be withdrawn at the last minute. Queers just couldn't get enough of a real man's dick, Jerry thought. But it was funny, he could usually spot faggots, and this guy was such a bad-ass, he looked like a truck driver or even a biker, maybe. I look more like a queer than he does, he thought, smoothing back the short sides of his hair and checking that the long top of his d.a. was still combed back, perfectly greased and in place. But that wasn't too funny, and the injustice of it, the implied accusation, made him determined to follow through with the cruise. Shit, he'd never come here again anyway, he just stopped here because it was close to her house and he needed a drink after being turned away from her door again. So he headed toward the john, giving a look over his shoulder to see if the other guy had noticed. Wouldn't the girls here just curl up and die if they knew what went on in the men's room?

The bathrooms were on opposite sides of a small hall. Jerry kicked open the door that said "Men" and inhaled the familiar, raunchy aroma. After two or three breaths you didn't notice the smell anymore. He kinda missed it. There were urinals along one wall, and some stalls. He really did need to pee. Let the fag come in the door while he had his cock out already; it would probably be a real treat for him. No reason why he, Jerry, should be the only one to get any fun out of it. Not that he was going to reciprocate or anything. He wasn't in high school anymore, for godsake.

Yeah, he really needed to piss, all right, but as he took his cock out, the familiar touch made it semirigid. His hand traveled up and down a couple of times in a lazy J/O gesture. Nothing was getting out of his bladder now. It almost hurt, being caught between two pleasures, anticipating both of them, not really able to enjoy either one.

Then somebody else kicked the door open, but this was different — it sounded like storm troopers. He turned, startled, and let go of his pants. They slipped down over his ass. The guy in the leather jacket was coming at him with a great big knife! Who did this mad fucker think he was, Rambo? He stumbled back, almost tripped on his pants, but the guy stepped on the loose end of a trouser leg, and Jerry pulled his feet free. His loafers went flying. Then a hand like a bear trap fastened on his shirtfront. "Hold still, boy," growled the mantrapper in his ear. The knife went between his shirt and his chest, and Jerry pulled away, frantic to keep that cold edge away from his suddenly hot skin. Ten inches of steel severed his shirt with one yank. He tried to get away, but was caught by the seat of his shorts — and those, too, were neatly severed and ripped off his body. He had long since lost his erection, and a sudden spurt of urine wet the rags that had been his underwear. He was completely naked. But before he could scream, a fistful of the shorts was stuffed in his mouth, and the knife was under his chin. One of his arms was bent and twisted behind his back, high enough to make him dance on tiptoe. "Spit that out and I'll cut your throat," the man said, and Jerry believed him.

He was turned around (amazing how quickly pain could make him obey) and quick-marched down the short, dark hallway (jeez, they ought to mop that floor), into an unlit parking lot, where gravel hurt his feet, up to a black van with oversized tires, a CB antenna, and customized flames curling around the windows and wheel wells. The man let go of his arm (but the sharp edge of steel kept his chin up), and released the side door of the van. Then the knife was gone, and he was shoved facedown onto the floor. "Put your hands between your ankles, fuck-face," his captor snarled, and he complied, even though it put his ass up in the air. There was a straight steel bar with four manacles on it — two big ones on the outside, two little ones on the inside — and his feet and wrists were put in the appropriate holes and the ratchets snapped shut.

"We got a long drive ahead of us," sneered the stranger. "This oughta take your mind off it." Something pointed and greasy intruded between the cheeks of Jerry's ass, and made him cry out. The cry loosened his bowels enough for the plug to lodge home, deep inside. Then it started to buzz. It must have a battery. This startled him so much he barely noticed the van had started rolling. Oh, fuck, this was the worst. He had never imagined anything like this ever hap-

171

pening to him. God, he had never been so scared or un-
happy — until he realized the vibrating butt-plug was giving
him an erection. At that, he cried. He hadn't cried since the
first time he went to camp. The other guys had made him
get out of his sleeping bag to join in a circle jerk. He was
the last one in the tent to come, so he had to eat his own
load in front of everybody.

He kept crying until his untouched, unloved cock pulsed
and he shot all over his own chest and belly. It was humiliating to come that way, all alone, being made to come by
an object he had no control over, worse even than jacking
off after a date with some cock-teasing bitch who let him
spend his money on her and then wouldn't put out. The only
good part of it was that the contractions of his orgasm pushed
the nasty rubber plug out of his ass. The cum dried slowly,
itching, shrinking, pulling his nipples in and making them
hard.

They had stopped moving. The door of the van slid open,
revealing a garage. The kidnapper clapped new irons on his
wrists and ankles, then released him from the bar. As he was
yanked out of the van, his tortured shoulder and neck muscles
cramped, and so did his calves. He screamed and almost fell.
But the man just picked him up, threw him over his shoulder,
unlocked a door, carried him down a flight of stairs, and
thrust him into a small cell. What kind of maniac has a real
jail cell, with real iron bars and a door that locks, in his
basement? The intense physical pain and the sudden con-
viction that he was going to be killed made Jerry break away
from the hand that steadied him. He began to shriek and

stumble around the cell. If his hands had not been manacled behind his back, he would have beat on the bars. He tried to kick over the cot. It was bolted to the floor.

"Good way to work the cramps out," said the stranger, and stepped out of the cell, turned a key, and left him alone with nothing but a single lightbulb (situated outside the cell, and protected with a strong wire cage) for company.

The rampage — such as it was — petered out pretty fast. In such a small space, with nothing to turn over or bust up — in fact, there was nothing in his environment that Jerry could have a significant effect upon — it did not relieve his feelings. He gave up and huddled on the cot for a while, but it was chilly in the cell, so he got up and began to pace, trying to keep warm.

He thought briefly of suicide. But how? There was no mirror to break. He had no belt, no shoelaces — not even a button to swallow! There were no sheets on the cot — just a thin mattress with a cover he could not tear with his fingers. There wasn't even a toilet to drown in! The only methods available (strangling himself with his chains, perhaps, or banging his head on the floor) would have required a force of character he simply did not possess.

His prowling led to only one major discovery — a drain in one corner of the cell. So he could piss without fouling his own nest. Good. But as soon as he had relieved this major discomfort, he becamse aware of two others — hunger and thirst. These torments kept him on his feet until he was so tired he fell onto the cot and slept.

He woke up terribly cold, stiff, with a bad headache and

an even worse taste in his mouth. He heard steps. The flight of stairs down to the basement was fairly long, and the man coming down them was taking his time. Instead of just waiting, he took a piss, but his urine was so concentrated that it burned. What was this guy going to do, watch him die slowly of dehydration? When he saw the big man standing outside his cell, one hand on his belt buckle, the other on a canteen slung over his shoulder, all the resentment turned into relief. Here, finally, was something new, some alternative to the boredom of his own companionship.

"Thirsty?"

"You know I am!"

"Want a drink, do you?"

"Yes!"

"Then ask for it with some manners, boy, and call me 'Sir.'"

"Wh ... wh ... I ... I will not!"

The dark brown eyes, under brows so bushy they met in the middle of the forehead, regarded him without a trace of impatience or anger. But there was also no compassion or remorse in that gaze. "Don't be stupid," he was told. "I got you locked up tighter than the president's rear end. There's no food and water in that cell. If you want any it has to come from me. So you just call me 'Sir' like a good boy and count yourself lucky I don't make you call me God. Because your life is in the palm of my hand."

"I ... can't ..."

The cap of the canteen was slowly unscrewed. It was

tilted. Precious water was about to be poured, wasted, onto the floor —

"Please! Sir! Let me have some water, Sir."

The cap was put back on the canteen, and the man moved menacingly toward the bars of his cell.

"But I said it, I said it, please, let me drink!"

"Oh, you'll get something to swallow, all right. Get down on your knees."

This was tricky to manage on a concrete floor, with no help from his hands, but he did it without hurting himself. His face was inches from the bars when a piece of sex-meat as dark as his captor's sun- and wind-burned face flopped into view and hit him on the cheek. He cringed. It was so much bigger than his own, and it wasn't clipped. The long foreskin, gathered at the tip of the cockhead in a soft pucker, made it seem even more alien. His captor skinned his dick, slowly, and Jerry felt gooseflesh go up his neck.

"This is the first thing I'm gonna feed you," the big man said. "Before anything else goes into your mouth, this does. That's how you earn your groceries. You better get used to it now because around here we eat three times a day. C'mon, boy, say, 'Thank you, Sir,' and kiss it."

Jerry's gorge rose, and he tried to back away, but his tender knees and short chains made him slow on the floor, and a callused paw darted through the bars, found his throat and squeezed it exactly the way it had squeezed a can of beer in the cowboy bar, so long ago.

"Whatsa matter, gorgeous?" (Squeeze, squeeze.) "You

couldn't take your eyes off my basket in that breeder bar." (Stroke, squeeze.) "What did you think I was taking you back to that toilet for?" (Extrahard grip, the edge of the hand felt like iron.) "You probably thought I was going to suck on *your* ding-dong, didn't ya, huh?" (A stroke hard enough to make him choke a little, a softer stroke.) "We just never know how things are going to turn out, do we?" (Both hands were around his neck, twisting in opposite directions.) "The universe just chews us up and spits us out." (Both hands, jacking off his throat.) "But you ain't going to spit *this* out." (Blunt, strong thumbs pressing in at the joints of his jaw, forced into the muscle until he cried with pain, and the cockhead slid between his lips and left a salty smear across his mouth. The taste of it, at least, was familiar, just like his own.)

For one split second, the smartest part of him whispered, "Suck it! You can't help it anymore than you can help kneeling on the floor or being cold and thirsty." But then pride and stupidity intervened (as was their habit) and he bit down on the deliciously resilient knob that was lodged in the hollow of his cheek. As soon as he had done it, he realized his mistake. It's the kind of thing you'd better do all the way or not at all. He had not anticipated how hard it would be to hurt another man's dick. His own ached with sympathy.

The cell door slammed open and suddenly he had more company than he dreamed would fit in such a small place — mad company, bad company. In two shakes of a dog's tail (or my tail, he thought bitterly), he was facedown on the cot. His ankle chain had been padlocked to the frame at the foot of the narrow bed, and it did not give him enough room to roll over. "You damn fool punk," the stranger said wearily, and took off his belt.

Every single blow hurt worse than the last. Not only was this man energetic and strong, but his strokes fell on a rather limited area — Jerry's butt and thighs. The broad, long garrison came down so hard it felt like a solid object rather than a flexible piece of leather. Jerry very quickly realized that sucking cock was not nearly as bad as this. Each blow had him rapidly revising his opinion of the relative merits of the two experiences — giving head and getting beaten — until he thought he'd rather deep-throat this man than go to heaven, if only it would stop the beating. The worst part of it was that he seemed to be saying all of this out loud, with a lot of "Sirs" and "please" and "I'll do anything you say" thrown in for good measure.

Still, it didn't stop until he had lost his breath and couldn't plead for mercy or call himself any more bad names. When it did stop, he was astonished by how little time had really elapsed. The Master (he had somehow become that in the dialogue that had accompanied the belting) was not even winded. Jerry looked at the man and his belt and his arm with new respect. When he was unchained he knelt by the side of the cot. "Thank you, Sir," he said and kissed the cock that was put to his dry lips. Then he opened his mouth. The hands were on his throat again, squeezing, and every time they eased their grip, the Master's cock went down his throat another inch. It was difficult but not awful. He arched his thighs and came up to get more of the rod. Just opening his mouth was not enough. He had to provide friction, traction. But it was hard to suck it and keep his teeth out of the way.

Above him, the Master was hissing, and one big fist was twisted in his forelock, practically banging his forehead against the muscular stomach, hard now with excitement and need. When his Master came, it was like having a hose down his throat that someone had suddenly turned on. It jerked as if it wanted to escape and sprayed hot thick stuff down his gullet. Somewhere, far away, another hose spurted sticky stuff over his thigh.

When he came to and realized he had come himself, once again without being touched, the fragile equilibrium he had achieved as a result of being beaten vanished, and he retched. The Master watched him crawl to the drain and attempt to be sick.

"Don't feel bad, shithead," he said, not unkindly. "You ain't the first piece of so-called trade I busted down to cocksucker. Knock that off and come rinse your mouth out."

The boy (as he was coming to think of himself) was not too far-gone to recognize common sense. He abandoned the stinking drain and crawled over to his Master, who shoved his big leg between Jerry's thighs and told him gruffly to lean against it. The first swallow of water was tipped delicately into his mouth. It was still cold and smelled deliciously of the metal canteen and its wet wool cover. After that, the water was poured from up higher, so he had to abandon the prop of his Master's thigh and open his mouth under it, like a dog drinking from a faucet.

Standing over the shackled body he had just possessed,

the Master said, "You got a lot of vanity, and it's all misplaced, boy. Whyncha try t'be proud of something you really can do — like let a big, fat dick tickle your tonsils? You're really good at that."

Then he was left alone and was glad because he was tired. The room was not so cold now. He slept. When he woke up, he realized he must have slept very deeply because he had not heard footsteps coming down the stairs. It was the smell of soup that woke him. There was a big bowl of it on the floor, in one of those fancy dog dishes that are weighted so they can't be tipped over. "That's smart," he thought. "I won't get it all over the floor." It was not until he was halfway through bolting down the wonderful stuff that he realized how low he had to be to think there was anything admirable or practical about eating from a dog bowl. But that didn't keep him from licking both the bowl and as much of his face as his tongue could reach, clean.

Then he realized he had a spectator. The Master wiped his face with a bandanna taken from his back pocket. "Good boy," he said. "You ready for another lesson?" Jerry was dubious. But the belt was safe in its loops, buckled, and no other weapons were in the Master's hands. "Maybe, Sir," he said. Sir laughed. "You don't have much choice, do you, boy?" "I don't have any choice, Sir," he said ruefully, as he was once more stretched stomach down on his cot and the ankle chain used to padlock him to it.

"Want some more water, boy?" He looked at the source of the offer. The Master had hung a bright red bag from the cell door and was offering him the nozzle. "Come on, it's clean, nothing but water," said the Master, and let a jet of it hit him in the face. Anything to delay the insertion of that nozzle where he knew it was meant to (and would) go. He opened his mouth and accepted a few swallows. Then the bag was taken off the door and his Master stuck his big cock into it. There was the unmistakable sound of somebody taking a healthy piss. "The enema du jour is prepared fresh daily," said the Master, and hung the bag back up. Jerry managed a weak smile.

"Before we do this," the Master said, "I think you ought to know that I'm not going to stop until I have exactly what I want from you." He lit a match on the sole of his boot, then slowly turned a big cigar in the flame. The cell was soon full of fragrant tobacco fumes. "We're being all cutesy right now but as soon as I do anything serious you're going to fight me again. I don't mind because I know I'll win. But it will make this easier on you if you know you're going to lose. Have you got any questions?"

"What are you going to do to me, Sir?"

"You're going to do anything I tell you to do and before much longer I won't have to tell you, you'll *know* what I want. But before we can reach that stage, I want to know everything about your sordid and misspent, snot-nosed youth. We're going to flush the past right out of you, starting now."

The nozzle was greased and inserted. "Just be glad it ain't my cigar — or something bigger," the Master chuckled. Then he wiggled some of the plastic tubing into his ass. Jerry squirmed. "Come t'think of it, you kinda like getting things shoved up your ass, don't you, pisspot? In fact, you creamed all over the floor of my van, didn't you? Now how do you suppose a straight boy learned how to do a trick like that, huh?"

There was a long, deadly silence. Jerry tentatively pulled on the ankle chain, but the pain was awful and the padlock was not going to pop open on his say-so. He would not answer the question. Not even to save himself a beating.

The Master sighed. "I think you ought to see some of my home movies," he said softly. From his cot, Jerry watched him leave the cell and click off the lights. There was the sound of another button being hit, a motor revving up — and film flashed on the back wall of the cell. The picture was large and grainy and so close he could barely see it, but the subject was so familiar that he didn't really need to watch it.

No wonder Caroline had always insisted on balling in her living room, on that big sofa. He was such a chump he never thought it was odd that she wouldn't take him into her bedroom. He just thought she couldn't wait to get some, had to have it the minute they walked in the door. She must have had a hidden camera set up in there, filming the whole thing. And, of course, the Master was the man he had accidentally discovered in her apartment.

She had Jerry on her lap. She was spanking him. How had she ever talked him into that? He had done something to make her call him a "bad boy" — oh, yeah, he wouldn't go down on her — and she had teased his prick enough to get him over her lap. (She had also had him by the balls, and had let him know — giggling — that she would hurt them if he did not do as she said.) Now she was putting a plug up his ass, rolling him over onto his back and poising herself over his erect cock, sinking down on it, holding his hands up over his head, playing with his nipples. The film had no sound, but he could remember the dialogue. "Who's fucking who now, little boy, huh? Who's fucking you? Can't you feel it up your ass? When I sit on your cock it moves it around. I've turned on the vibrator, it's going to make you come, it's my cock that's going to make you come."

The Master released the clamp on the enema tube, and water started to flow into him. He was allowed to use a bedpan, then made to bend over for another dose of water-and-piss, all in the ghastly flickering light of these movies, made of the stuff of shame. He had been so stupid then. He had excused everything she did to him on the grounds that she was a horny, older woman who was so hot for him, she couldn't help but go overboard expressing her lust. Now he saw the truth. Caroline had picked him up, initiated him into a series of demeaning and subservient acts (the film showed her shoe in his face, the long and dangerous heel going in and out of his mouth), and he had not resisted or protested. In fact, it was the best sex he had ever had.

Another session on the bedpan, more water. He was fascinated by the sight of her putting clips on his nipples, clips that were connected by a chain. Now she was tying his cock up. The long ends of the leather laces were brought up and secured to the tit clamps. And the harder she pulled, the harder he got. The Master's hands fastened on his teats, hauled on them — rougher, more comforting than Caroline's sharp nails. He was lying on his back on the cot now. He didn't know if he was still watching the movie or just re- playing memories in his mind. Clamps (identical to those in the film) were fastened on his nipples. He felt leather lace being wound around his cock and balls. The inevitable du- plication — lace tied around chain, both pulled until he came up off the bed, hard between the legs, his balls swollen to bursting point, aching for more pain if it meant more sex, more stimulation for his cock, more intense release. Release from that woman, that awful, wicked, vengeful woman who had gone to so much trouble to get him into permanent trouble.

Damn her, damn her, he brought his knees up as his Master climbed onto the foot of the bed. He was wearing leather chaps, a leather jacket; nothing else. As the Master bent over Jerry to unlock his wrist chains, the boy kissed his chest, rubbed his face into the coarse fur, grateful for the lack of perfume, the presence of hard muscle instead of soft breasts. He barely noticed the weight that rested on his well- clamped tits as the Master reached for the head of the bed and refastened his hands to it, so they were no longer pinned underneath his body. He was too busy sucking on those nipples, nipples that were not in pain; it was his job to give them pleasure while his own suffered. It was his vocation.

The laces kept his cock out of the way as a hand full of lubricant spread him, speared him, went where the nozzle and warm water and piss had prepared a way. He was clean inside and smooth, open to the touch, but always clinging, providing a snug fit for the fingers that stroked him, longing to retain them and love them and keep them inside, where they gave him so much pleasure that he gasped, choked on his desire as the fingers were withdrawn. Restlessly, he moved his slippery ass so the ring of muscle lodged against the head of the cock that was being pointed at it, and absorbed it. The whole length of the thing inside him throbbed. This was not a piece of plastic, it was flesh, man flesh, like his own only free, free to use him. (And once again it was his task, his calling, to pleasure a part of his Master while his own, equivalent part was hurting.) There was a little pain around his opening, a feeling of something resisting then being broken, and he wanted it to be broken so he could experience everything fully, without resistance, without pride, meet thrust with thrust and groan into the same mouth that covered his and groaned.

"Fuck me, Sir, please, fuck me harder," he begged and got his wish. He could not come because of the binding around his cock, and he was glad, because he wanted to be a vessel, receive; he had fucked everything up, made a mess of it all, couldn't control or manage or direct things; it was better to get fucked, to be controlled, to be shown how his body responded automatically to this touch, this stroke, this degree of dilation and penetration and be rubbed here inside, there, the feelings kept changing and growing, how could he feel so much and still feel more and not explode or be damaged or destroyed?

His torso was imprisoned between arms that bulged with the strain of holding up a big man's body during a full-out fuck. He turned his head and kissed the arms, licked them, tried to get his fettered hands down far enough to caress them. "Tell me," Sir gritted, "what a little shit you are."

There was no time for a full confession. He knew Sir would extract all the details: The faggots he enticed and then rolled (and what really happened between him and the men he did not rob). The jobs he had botched with petty thievery or laziness. The women who had treated him with almost as much contempt as he felt for them. The physique magazines and where he hid them and what he did in the stores where he bought them. For now it was enough to just say, "I *am* a piece of shit, this is all I'm good for, I have to have your cock in me, please, please, please, Sir, please."

The cock went in and in again, meeting no resistance, but the lining of his ass had been roughened somewhat, giving the fuck a new texture, a slight edge. "I belong to you!" he cried, and with a sharp jerk, the Master released the cock-laces and let the slave's jism spill between them. "I belong to you!" Jerry continued to cry, even after his cock ran dry. After all, his Master's tool was still at work, and that was the only thing that mattered. A wolf's grin split the Master's black beard. Caroline had kept her promise — with a little help from her big brother.

The projector ran out of film and the loose end of celluloid flapped like a scarecrow in the wind, but the two of them never noticed they were fucking in the pure white light of an empty screen.

NEEDLESS TO SAY

Lisa Palac

•

The frozen vegetable display made Angelique's nipples hard. She was choosing between a carton of chopped spinach and a bag of carrots, broccoli and cauliflower otherwise known as California Medley.

California . . . California. Just the sound of the word made her wet. The home of indigenous blonde bimbos and vacant surfer dudes who drenched themselves in various pore-clogging palm oils, then panted like rabid dogs as they slid around the back seat of their cherry '77 Cutlass convertibles. The acme of hot-tub orgies with big dicks from the Hollywood Hills, cellular phone sex and fuchsia teddies with nipple cut-outs. The Land of Porn.

Angelique dreamed of performing incredibly nasty acts on a Naugahyde couch while the videotape rolled. She and some greased-up stud would pump and munch on each other like snacks, eventually sliding down onto the lime shag carpet, while the slightly balding director with a roll of fat hanging over his Elvis — The King! abalone belt buckle shouted, "That's it BAYbee! Show it all to me BAYbee! Ye-he-hes!"

She could make the Oooh Yeah Face better than Ginger Lynn and she could be making a million fucking dollars at it too, but it wasn't going to happen in Milwaukee.

Angelique threw the bag of frozen nuggets on top of the bratwurst. Her high heels clicked against the waxed checkerboard floor of Giuseppe's Finer Foods as she pushed the shopping cart down the aisle, wiggling her ass seductively for all of her regulars to see. She could make those pimply-faced, nervous stock boys cream in their pants if she wanted to. All that teenage testosterone ready to explode like a nuclear warhead at the mere sight of a pubic hair. Out of the corner of her eye, Angelique could see them straining to keep their eyes glued to her luscious ass.

She wore her favorite red cha-cha heels today and they made her butt stand out like a ripe bubble. Her legs were longer than Route 66 with directions to the Tunnel of Love posted every mile. The leopard lycra spandex skirt barely covered her back door and a cut-off T-shirt revealed that her man-made 34C tits didn't need a bra. A turgid mass of bleach-blonde hair, glued in place by an entire can of Aqua-Net Firm Hold, shot up toward the ceiling, then fell around her shoulders. Her eyes were circled with tons of thick black eyeliner and her lips were colored California Orange.

Wiggle it, Angie. She bent over just a little bit, pretending to check something in the cart, and rotated her firm cheeks. Surreptitiously, she glanced over her shoulder just in time to catch the stock boys turn their drooling faces back to a freezer full of frozen food.

Bending over wasn't the only talent she had. She knew all the poses from grinding along with Tony's (her now ex-boyfriend and total jerk) porno tapes and thumbing through copies of all his *fucking* fuck magazines. Next to laughing at the homemade Polaroids of all the flabby-assed sluts in the swingers' section, Angelique liked the letters from readers the best, and was dying to know if they were real. They were always saying things like, "The two virgin pizza delivery girls, needless to say, were begging to suck my cock!" or "Needless to say, I shot my biggest load watching her screw my brother and his Latvian lesbian Bingo tutor in the tool shed!" If these letters were real, then why didn't something like that happen to her? Why, why, why? Her bottom lip began to curl down into a little pout. She could screw in a tool shed better than any other Slavic lesbo, if she only had half a chance. Life was so unfair.

To cheer herself up, she wheeled the cart into the Shampoo/Toothpaste/Feminine Hygiene aisle. For Angelique, shopping was a confession of faith; a cold cash belief that the proper combination of fake tan, garter belts and the right deodorant would ultimately lead her to Porn Star status. Or at least the simulated adventures of one.

Angie Lee flipped on her Walkman. How do they expect people to have a meaningful shopping experience when the air is filled with this nauseating Muzak? she thought.

I'm burnin' up, burnin' up for your luh-uv . . .

Madonna's breathy squeals blasted through the wires.
This crotch-grabbing, mattress-humping, Catholic Italian
who liked to be spanked was Angelique's absolute idol. Angie
had all her records, but her favorite was still the first one.
"Burnin' Up" was her manifesto and The Boy Toy, her fearless leader. That woman had balls . . . and great tits, too.
Angelique wondered what kind of douche she used.

She sang along with the superstar. She shook her head
with such raging abandon, her hair actually moved. She
pranced down the aisle, submersed in a distorted MTV wet
dream.

*. . . I'll do anything, I'm not the same, I have no shame . . . I'm
on FIRE!*

The music pounded away like an insatiable hard-on, while
her eyes scanned the myriad products available for today's
woman: feminine deodorant sprays, suppositories, intimate
cleansers, disposable douches and douche bags; maxi pads,
mini-pads, tampons on a stick and tampons on a string; pills
to avoid bloating, crabbiness, over-eating, pimple-produc-
tion, fatigue, iron deficiency, depression, moodiness and tem-
per tantrums, which when unchecked could lead to frenzied
fits of murder!

C'mon let go!

Madonna was insistent. The vocals ripped apart Angelique's hesitation and with a sweeping motion, she dumped
the entire shelf into her cart. Shit, she broke a nail.

The cart was overflowing with goodies now. Time to go.
Happily, she made her way toward the check-out. Okay,

was she obsessing? Maybe there was one box too many of panty shields. Maybe she should wear two at a time. One time Tony asked her why a chick would need to wear a pad everyday.

"I thought that thing only happened once a month, unless ya got knocked up or somethin'. Whaddaya get? Some fuckin' clam disease? Haw, haw, haw." Stupid asshole.

Or the time when Tony was laid off from the meat-packing plant and he listened to those Springsteen records all fuckin' day and would whip out his cock whenever some ugly babe got rejected on "Love Hook-Up," the dial-a-date show.

"Come and get it, Fido! Here, Barky!" he'd say, dangling his dick in front of the TV and swallowing a pisswarm Meister Brau.

What a low-class scum-sucking shit. He thought he was so great, and he didn't even know he had pimples on his ass and left skid marks in his underwear. Breaking up with him was the smartest thing she ever did — besides buying those refrigerator magnets on sale.

No matter what line Angelique picked, it always turned out to be the longest one. There was always some old lady who picked an item without a price tag or insisted on digging for exact change in the bottom of her purse. To help the century pass, Angie grabbed the latest issue of *Charm* magazine and scanned the headlines on the cover: Where Men Like to be Licked, Lipstick Tricks, Bolivian Fashion Rage, Money: How to Get It, Find Your G-Spot in Minutes. She had a few minutes. She flipped to page 53.

She rested her elbows on the rail of the cart and arched her back so that her succulent plumbutt stuck way out. She slid off one high heel and slowly began to rub her bare foot against the inside of her other leg as she began reading the sexy instructions. Wash hands . . . two fingers . . . insert deeply . . . pressing forward . . . may feel like a small almond. Angelique pressed her creamy thighs together and gave a teensy little moan. She drew the magazine closer to her, shielding her face with the glossy pages. Gingerly, she ran one finger around the outline of her wet pink lips, then drove it into her mouth like a garden spike. She rammed one finger, then two, in and out of her lip service until they were completely covered in her sweet stickiness. She was just about to try and sneak them down to her pussy when she noticed the spy.

Two lines over Angel saw Mrs. Alfaromeo. She kept glancing and pointing at Angelique, then whispering to her prune-faced old man. That nosy bitch, thought Angel, everybody probably knows about my abortion now. Mrs. Alfaromeo's daughter, Carmella, worked at the clinic and provided the entire neighborhood with abortion gossip. Somebody should gag that prissy little Carmella I-Have-No-Cunt.

Mrs. Alfaromeo was now smiling and waving and flapping her gums frantically; obviously trying to cover up her spying blunder with some forced conversation.

Angel lowered the magazine and pulled the headphones away from her ears.

"What," Angie gave her best Bored Bitch imitation, "are you saying?"

"I say, how you feeling?"

Fuck. She knows. Angelique gave the geriatric an indignant stare.

"I feel pretty horny after watching your daughter give some black guy a blow-job on your front proch last night!"

The old woman took a big swallow of air and slammed a can of tomato paste down on the conveyor belt with deliberate rage. She prayed to the fluorescent ceiling lights and told her wrinkled porker that he should have worn his hearing aid if he wanted to know what was going on. Smiling, Angel flung the magazine in with the other treats, pushed her cart up to the register, and began unpiling her load.

Angelique couldn't resist flashing the bag boy. She made sure to give him a good view of her braless silicone wonders with every item she placed on the moving black belt. *You want a show, honey?* she thought, *I'll give it to you and you can pay me later.*

"Total's 83.94." The gum-chomping check-out girl was barely understandable.

Angie Lee tried to focus on counting her cash, but couldn't keep her eyes off the nubile flesh who was just finishing packing up the paper bags with the last box of vaginal suppositories. She imagined the growing desire in his pants and licked her lips in anticipation.

"That's 83.94."

She made the transaction and slung her purse over her shoulder. Meanwhile the pulsing behemoth put the bags into an empty cart, preparing for their departure.

"I need some help puttin' all this stuff in my car." Oh, Angie you coy bitch. "Could you help me?"

"Sure," he said. Wasn't he sweet? A little bit of acne but great hair.

He followed Angie out into the parking lot. Click, click, click. Her plastic heels tapped the black tar surface.

She made sure to walk in front of him, not beside him, so that he could revel in her perfect *perfect* ass. She also wanted to give him the opportunity to rub up against her when she bent over to slam the key in the lock. But he didn't take the bait when she opened up the trunk of her 1989 Buick Riviera. What the hell was this throbbing glob of hormones waiting for?

She spun around and slammed her lips into his. Snatching a fistful of his crusty gelled hair, she slurped and slobbered all over his adolescent face, smearing it with California Orange. Her tongue desperately searched for the way into his love-licker, but he would not open his mouth.

"Open your mouth, baby," Angie Lee cooed. "Open up for Mommy."

The bag boy stood motionless. His face was more frozen than the bag of California Medley, which was now melting in the suffocating Wisconsin sun. Only his eyes were bulging.

"Lamby-pie, open your mouth and let my slippery snake in," she hissed. Still no response. "I said open it, you little shit!" Angie yanked his bottom lip down with one hand and pried his teeth apart with the other. Her pointy tongue darted

193

in and out of his cavity-filled mouth with a winner-take-all fury. And this conquest was only the beginning.

She began grinding and writhing against his filthy green Giuseppe's apron. Her hungry crotch humped his leg while she grabbed his ass with both hands and pounded his scared stiff body against her loose slutty self. She clawed at his face with her painted talons and dug her teeth into his never-been-kissed flesh.

"Owww!' he screamed. The sound of his sudden yelp made her lose her balance and she practically twisted her ankle when her cha-cha heel gave way.

"Damn it you lovely little virgin bastard, you hot horny teen-ager," she whispered into his waxy ear, "I'm going to rip you up."

Angie Lee stuffed her sex plans into his brain. Detailed descriptions of coital exploits were flooding his head, but bag boy had a one track mind: If he didn't get back soon, he'd lose his fifteen-minute break. With anxious tenacity his head kept snapping back in the direction of the grocery store, straining to see who might be witnessing his possible de-flowerment, until Angelique put the iron grip on his boner-to-be.

"I am a bitch in heat!" she cried, enunciating every word like a Pentacostal preacher. "And you're gonna cool me off." In a smooth move, she caught his crumpled black tie and dragged him around to the side of the car.

He was flat on his back in the back seat when Angie ripped off her T-shirt and produced two perfect melons.

Straddling him, she began playing with her overripe fruits, making little circles around her rock hard nipples.

"Aren't you dying to touch me?" Sugar poured out of her mouth. "Aren't you . . . ?" She paused, eyebrows raised, waiting for his name.

"Sergio . . . but . . . uhm . . . like my friends call me Sam."

"Oooo Sam. I like Sam. Oooo, yeah." She tweaked her nipples harder and harder and sucked in a lot of air every time she said Oooo, yeah. Just like in the movies.

She reached out and tugged on his zipper, but he grabbed her wrist.

"What's the matter, Sammy?"

"You're not sick or anything are you? I mean you bought all that weird stuff."

Suddenly her eyes narrowed into evil slits. "What *weird* stuff?" She spit the words out through her clenched teeth, now just inches away from his petrified face.

"All that stuff, for like when girls get infections."

"I don't have any infections. All of that *stuff* keeps me smelling fresh and feminine. You want me to be feminine, don't you?"

"Yeah . . . I guess so."

"Tell me what else you want." He shrugged his shoulders. "I'll tell you what you want! You want my honey pot! My carnal canal! My shaved slice of sin! MY PUSSY!" Her fingernails tore into his stained white bag-boy shirt, releasing a shower of buttons.

"You want to see my cunt riding up and down on your virginal cock, don't you? You want to see me rub my clit? Do you know what that is? My clit? I bet you don't, you naive slave-boy. See, Oooo I'm rubbing it now. Oooo yeah. Ooooh oooh ooooh you want to hear me scream when I come and keep on screaming as I take more and more of your thick pud deep deep and deeper inside me. You want to see me explode again when you shoot hot lava blasts from your volcanic rod deep inside my mammoth crater! Don't you? Oooo yeah, oh here it comes baby, here it comes! I'm showin' it to you, baby! Oh! Oh! Oh! OOOOooo YEAH!"

She heard the buzz droning in the distance. Her vibrator must have gone off accidentally in her purse, she thought. She opened her eyes. Instead, it was the annoying signal telling her the car door was ajar. He was gone.

She adjusted the rear view mirror and checked her lipstick at the same time. Some idiot behind her was beeping their horn. The light was green. Fuck you, asshole. She gave him the finger. Her tires squealed when she rammed the pedal to the floor. In her mind, she was already composing the letter: "I was doing my weekly shopping, when this totally gorgeous stock boy, who was also a virgin, offered to take my groceries out to the car. He ended up packing my trunk in more ways than one! Needless to say, I never thought it could happen to me. . . ."

THE FLOOD

Ronald Sukenick

·

I. The Fifth Force

The Uncles used to tell a story about two business men who find themselves in adjacent deck chairs in Miami Beach. "So what do you do?" asks one.

"I'm retired," he says. "I had a fire that wrecked my store, so I took the insurance money and I came down here."

"The same thing happened with me," says the other. "I had a flood that ruined my store so I took the insurance and retired."

"A flood?" says the other man. "How do you start a flood?"

With Austyn, Sergio Biennale starts a flood.

She meets him at a dinner in Rue de la Tombe Issoire. Biennale is an avant-garde music maestro as well as an impressario who knows how to orchestrate business and art.

He specializes in the new electronic music and has a scientific theory about the essence of sound. Biennale analyzes music as waves of vibrating electrons that are as much a matter of pure matter as a piece of meat. Music is simply a process of liberating energy from mass, a process that can be accomplished as well by a computer as by a human brain. Better, because more precise.

And once energy is released from the mass it floods all systems, overwhelming them and forcing them to establish new connections.

This does not merely pertain to music. It pertains to politics, for example. And to sex.

"Therefore," says Biennale, "I base my music on scientific principles. I am programming my computers to compose a suite based on the four fundamental forces of the universe — the strong force, the weak force, magnetic force and the force of gravity."

"You're getting the fifth force," says Ron.

"What's that?"

"The force of levity, that counterbalances the force of gravity, and that's essential for the continuation of sentient life in a universe of inert matter."

"Your friend is a comedian," Biennale says to Austyn.

"Perhaps he thinks so."

Ron is aware that five minutes after they're introduced they're chattering like machine guns in a way that makes it clear they don't want to be interrupted by anyone. Biennale has an attractive presence. He manages to project an air of

Italian insouciance that does not undermine an almost Wagnerian seriousness. Tall, blond, blue eyed and rugged, he has a regularity of features marred only by a curious birth mark on his forehead roughly suggesting some alphabetical character.

When Ron asks Austyn about Biennale after they get home she just gives him one of those totally contemptuous stares.

Right after that Austyn starts going out every afternoon. She says she's working on a project at the music computer center. Wherever she's going, Ron can't help noticing that every evening she comes back in a happier mood. Great. The thought crosses his mind that she's getting it on with Biennale but as far as he's concerned at this point she could be getting it on with the Eiffel Tower as long as it improves her mood.

Austyn is wired. Biennale must whip her to frenzy. One evening she comes home with her ass so black and blue she can't sit down without a cushion. She says she fell down. She must have fallen down very thoroughly. Ron knows for a fact that Biennale leaves town about a week after he first meets Austyn, so their sex scene had to be brief. But it apparently starts a flood, a torrent of demonic energy in Austyn that Ron finds startling. She's transformed into some kind of diabolic dynamo.

It occurs to Ron that what she's always needed is to be whipped into the harness of some arduous task. It turns out after several weeks that she's going into business. The culture business.

You heard no doubt of the Do-It-Yourself Symphony fad of some years ago? Or the Do-It-Yourself Sonnet? That was Austyn. So also was the Do-It-Yourself Short Story and the Do-It-Yourself Masterpiece. Even the Do-It-Yourself Novel. Etcetera. The notion is surprisingly simple, if derivative. It comes out of the old avant garde idea of excerpting portions of any art work and then recombining them to get a new work.

Austyn's inspiration is to computerize the process. So you stick your Do-It-Yourself Symphony program in your PC, play around with it a little bit till you get some instant Beethoven, or Stravinsky, or any combination thereof, record it on tape and bore your friends with it.

You wouldn't believe the entrepreneurial effort that went into this project. If Austyn weren't a millionaire, she probably would have become a millionaire. Unfortunately the project was a little ahead of affordable technology, but she sold the idea for a tidy sum and kicked off her career in the home entertainment business.

The interesting thing for Ron to watch is that the more she gets involved in her business the less she's interested in sensuality. As she becomes a dynamo in work she becomes almost virginal in sex. It's as if Austyn is now complete in herself and doesn't need anyone else. As if she's now a whole person.

But now that Austyn is a whole person, there's something missing, something she had before that she doesn't have now, that Ron is hard put to define.

It's like what she had before was exactly something missing, something that she was struggling hard to find.

Now that she's found it it's a little anti-climactic.

Ron used to sense a tension in her, a potentially fertile anxiety. He had the sense about her that he never knew what she was going to do next that was the key factor in his attraction to her. He used to find her open ended, pun intended, and her open end excited him. Now she's more like a closed whole. But a whole that's missing something. An unwhole whole.

Ron suspects even then that the fact that she's become unwholly whole is Biennale's influence. Because he already thinks Biennale is a fake, as close to an empty whole as he believes anybody can get. He suspects that Biennale in some way has communicated to her a social disease through the medium of culture. A culture is a medium that does not merely foster the saving genius of a people, a culture also grows germs that can destroy the culture itself.

Biennale's effect on Austyn is to transform her from an interesting failure to a boring success.

Ron realizes that Biennale must have taught Austyn the rules of the game. And he senses that the rules of the game are not Jewish rules.

It's around this time that Ron's relation with Austyn disintegrates totally and he sees that they have to split.

But this episode gives Ron his first real clue about how the virus is communicated. This is when he decides to drop everything else and concentrate on his research.

II. *Adults Only*

Ron senses that Austyn's problem with him, and probably his with her, is that they're too much alike. Despite all appearances they are both afflicted with a certain innocence, an unworldliness in the way they deal with the world, almost as if the world doesn't really exist.

In what strange realm do they live, you have to wonder.

Even their vices have an air of artifice, as if they are something learned from books. The similarity is almost familial.

At some level they are both aware of this unworldliness and despise it. Life seems to be a disease they yearn to catch.

In Ron this results in a pursuit of vulgarity. Austyn on the other hand craves the intrusion of the alien, a penetration by the banal. Thus her desire for violation is much deeper than masochism.

The consequence of this syndrome for Austyn is a tendency to compromising situations and outrageous behavior.

If you are under twenty-one or easily shocked you probably should not read what follows. Unless you are accompanied by an adult or have a note from your shrink.

Ron can't say for sure, but based on some of the comments Austyn drops and a bit on his own imagination, this is how he thinks Biennale domesticates her demons.

Austyn goes to meet Biennale to talk to him about her avant-garde music project. She thinks he might be just the man to conduct her on-stage computer performance to its desired crescendo. And he quickly recognizes in her usual domineering impertinence a polar need to be subdued and broken. Just his meat.

Of course Biennale is very accommodating. But he insists first of all on a series of rehearsals. Anything else would be less than professional. He says he'd like to make sure the project is marketable, and if it isn't, redirect it toward a targetted audience. He says even culture has a bottom line. He quotes Robert Frost saying that everything has to come to market.

Austyn has a strong intuition that Biennale is the worst kind of sexist pig. But maybe even because of that, she feels a certain erotic curiosity. In any case, always practical, she acquiesces.

He begins by asking her to disrobe according to his precise instructions, while he sits in an easy chair and picks his teeth. Then he directs her through a series of gynecological maneuvers such as standing in front of him hefting her breasts, lying on a table in an obstetrical posture, masturbating for a while. His instructions have an exactness that's almost clinical.

At the end of this phase of the rehearsal he takes her temperature. Rectally, of course. He notes that it's starting to rise. Above normal.

Then gradually, judiciously, Biennale begins to caress her here and there, staying carefully away from the erogenous zones at first, but slowly shifting his attention to her lips, her nipples, her thighs, her rectum, her vagina. Then he starts with a vibrator. When he sees she's ready to come he starts applying his tongue, first to her nipples then her clitoris. At the first sign of the spasm he stops. Naturally she's horribly disappointed and asks him why. Instead of answering he makes her get down on her knees and lick his penis. It's possible at this point that he breaks out the whip, teaches her to beg.

This phase goes on for a while with repetitions, there's no need to get into the fat and gristle. In fact the details are the same, it's only the intensity of the experience that Biennale keeps increasing notch by notch. Suffice it to say that Biennale continues until he sees that she's a completely volitionless piece of needy meat, squirming helplessly under his ministrations.

By this point Austyn realizes what's happening to her. She's being domesticated. Trained.

Then Biennale starts making her come. As soon as she's finished with one orgasm he begins preparing her for the next, stimulating her with a frightening physiological accuracy. He does not, of course, use his penis, not at first. He uses his finger, his tongue, the tip of his boot, the end of a candle, a vibrator and even a small eggplant that happens to hand.

He threatens to use his penis. That is, he inserts the tip, rubs it around a bit, and then withdraws, substituting some other object in its place. Ron uses the word threatens because it has to be said that BIENNALE'S COCK IS HUGE, actually capable of inspiring a kind of titillated fear of impending penetration in the maidens who are conscious that they are about to experience its throbbing purple alien amplitude inside their bodies. To give you some idea, when

Austyn sucks it, she can only get the very tip of the glans in her mouth and has to content herself with licking the rest. And she has a big mouth.

(Ron knows the doctrine is that size is not a significant factor, but Ron's female informants persist in reporting it is.)

In fact, when Austyn first sees Biennale's cock erect spring out as he unzips his fly she recoils from it as from a jack-in-the-box. Her first, frightened thought is that it will never fit. And it's not as if the thing looks like it can flex and accommodate to a different size or shape — no, it looks like a rigid shaft of purple-veined marble. And yet when he penetrates her with it he knows how to rub, and probe, and slowly stretch so that it suddenly slides in with a minimum amount of, yes, pain, but an overwhelming sensation of pleasure. And of this thick, leaden column of pulsing meat Biennale has perfect knowledge. He is totally in control of his instrument. With the result that he can maintain it indefinitely within Austyn's writhing body as her spasms mount one on top of the next, wave after wave, until she subsides not for lack of further desire but of sheer carnal exhaustion.

"I'm all fucked out," she tells him. Lying there, sensuously limp, it flashes through Austyn's mind that she doesn't even like Biennale. But simultaneously she realizes that it doesn't matter that she doesn't like him and that not liking him even makes the pleasure he forces her to have more excruciatingly acute. She realizes he's made himself her master and you're not supposed to like your master or, rather, it's irrelevant.

Biennale immediately senses in her muscle tone a certain limp obedience, a surrender, a total submissiveness. He knows she's been broken. Only then does Biennale allow himself to come, shooting extravagant gouts of hot sperm into her shuddering womb, forcing her to come yet one more shattering time.

It's at this precise instant, Ron supposes, that Biennale communicates the virus to her, for the first time uncensored and unabridged. And she's grateful for it. She's not only grateful for the pleasure he's given her, but also for the pleasure she's been able to give him.

What Austyn doesn't understand about Biennale is that he has no pleasure in sex. He'd just as well eat a steak as fuck a woman, just as well take a shit as get an erection, just as well sneeze as come. For him it's a pure power trip.

From that moment on Austyn has only one gut level desire governing her psyche, an unwholesome craving to be mastered or, failing that, an urge to master others.

It's clear to both Austyn and Biennale that henceforth they can make music together. Computer or no computer.

From here on though, Austyn's commitment to culture begins to split. The performance side of her project, formerly self-expressive, turns into a powerful dynamic of consumer exploitation. The avant-garde side, after she stops rehearsing with Strop, turns passive, inert, virginal, an experiment in the purity of masturbation, ultimately concerning only her own psyche.

NINETY-THREE MILLION MILES AWAY

Barbara Gowdy

·

At least part of the reason Ali married Claude, a cosmetic surgeon with a growing practice, was so that she could quit her boring government job. Claude was all for it. "You only have one life to live," he said. "You only have one kick at the can." He gave her a generous allowance and told her to do what she wanted.

She wasn't sure what that was, aside from trying on clothes in expensive stores. Claude suggested something musical — she loved music — so she took dance classes and piano lessons and discovered that she had a tin ear and no sense of rhythm. She fell into a mild depression during which she peevishly questioned Claude about the ethics of cosmetic surgery.

"It all depends on what light you're looking at it in,"

Claude said. He was not easily riled. What Ali needed to do, he said, was take the wider view.

She agreed. She decided to devote herself to learning, and she began a regime of reading and studying, five days a week, five to six hours a day. She read novels, plays, biographies, essays, magazine articles, almanacs, the New Testament, *The Concise Oxford Dictionary, The Harper Anthology of Poetry.*

But after a year of this, although she became known as the person at dinner parties who could supply the name or date that somebody was snapping around for, she wasn't particularly happy, and she didn't even feel smart. Far from it, she felt stupid, a machine, an idiot savant whose one talent was memorization. If she had any *creative* talent, which was the only kind she really admired, she wasn't going to find it by armoring herself with facts. She grew slightly paranoid that Claude wanted her to settle down and have a baby.

A few days before their second wedding anniversary she and Claude bought a condominium apartment with floor-to-ceiling windows, and Ali decided to abandon her reading regime and to take up painting. Since she didn't know the first thing about painting or even drawing, she studied pictures from art books. She did know what her first subject was going to be — herself in the nude. Several months earlier she'd had a dream about spotting her signature in the corner of a painting, and realizing from the conversation of the men who were admiring it (and blocking her view) that it was an extraordinary rendition of her naked self. She took the dream to be a sign. For several weeks she studied the proportions, skin tones and muscle definitions of the nudes in her books, then she went out and bought art supplies and a self-standing, full-length mirror.

She set up her work area in the middle of the living room. Here she had light without being directly in front of the window. When she was all ready to begin, she stood before the mirror and slipped off her white terry-cloth housecoat and her pink flannelette pajamas, letting them fall to the floor. It aroused her a little to witness her careless shedding of clothes. She tried a pose: hands folded and resting loosely under her stomach, feet buried in the drift of her housecoat.

For some reason, however, she couldn't get a fix on what she looked like. Her face and body seemed indistinct, secretive in a way, as if they were actually well-defined, but not to her, or not from where she was looking.

She decided that she should simply start, and see what happened. She did a pencil drawing of herself sitting in a chair and stretching. It struck her as being very good, not that she could really judge, but the out-of-kilter proportions seemed slyly deliberate, and there was a pleasing simplicity to the reaching arms and the elongated curve of the neck. Because flattery hadn't been her intention, Ali felt that at last she may have wrenched a vision out of her soul.

The next morning she got out of bed unusually early, not long after Claude had left the apartment, and discovered sunlight streaming obliquely into the living room through a gap between their building and the apartment house next door. As far as she knew, and in spite of the plate-glass windows, this was the only direct light they got. Deciding to make use of it while it lasted, she moved her easel, chair, and mirror closer to the window. Then she took off her housecoat and pajamas.

For a few moments she stood there looking at herself, wondering what it was that had inspired the sketch. Today she was disposed to seeing herself as not bad, overall. As far as certain specifics went, though, as to whether her breasts were small, for instance, or her eyes close together, she remained in the dark.

Did other people find her looks ambiguous? Claude was always calling her beautiful, except that the way he put it — "You're beautiful to me," or "I think you're beautiful" — made it sound as if she should understand that his taste in women was unconventional. Her only boyfriend before Claude, a guy called Roger, told her she was great but never said how exactly. When they had sex, Roger liked to hold the base of his penis and watch it going in and out of her. Once, he said that there were days he got so horny at the office, his pencil turned him on. She thought it should have been his pencil sharpener.

She covered her breasts with her hands. Down her cleavage a drop of sweat slid haltingly, a sensation like the tip of a tongue. She circled her palms until her nipples hardened, and imagined a man's hands . . . not Claude's — a man's hands not attached to any particular man. She looked out the window.

In the apartment across from her she saw a man.

She leapt to one side, behind the drapes. Her heart pounded violently, but only for a moment, as if something had thundered by, dangerously close. She wiped her wet forehead on the drapes, then, without looking at the window, walked back to her easel, picked up her palette and brush, and began to mix paint. She gave herself a glance in the mirror, but she had no intention of trying to duplicate her own skin tone. She wanted something purer. White with just a hint of rose, like the glance of color in a soap bubble.

Her strokes were short and light to control dripping. She liked the effect, though . . . how it made the woman appear as if she were covered in feathers. Paint splashed on her own skin, but she resisted putting her smock on. The room seemed preternaturally white and airy; the windows beyond the mirror gleamed. Being so close to the windows gave her the tranced sensation of standing at the edge of a cliff.

A few minutes before she lost the direct sun, she finished the woman's skin. She set down her palette and put her brush in turpentine, then wet a rag in the turpentine and wiped paint off her hands and where it had dripped on her thighs and feet. She thought about the sun. She thought that it is ninety-three million miles away and that its fuel supply will last another five billion years. Instead of thinking about the man who was watching her, she tried to recall a solar chart she had memorized a couple of years ago.

The surface temperature is six thousand degrees Fahrenheit, she told herself. Double that number, and you have how many times bigger the surface of the sun is compared to the surface of the earth. Except that because the sun is a ball of hot gas, it actually has no surface.

When she had rubbed the paint off herself, she went into

the kitchen to wash away the turpentine with soap and water. The man's eyes tracked her. She didn't have to glance at the window for confirmation. She switched on the light above the sink, soaped the dishcloth, and began to wipe her skin. There was no reason to clean her arms, but she lifted each one and wiped the cloth over it. She wiped her breasts. She seemed to share in his scrutiny, as if she were looking at herself through his eyes. From his perspective she was able to see her physical self very clearly — her shiny, red-highlighted hair, her small waist and heart-shaped bottom, the dreamy tilt to her head.

She began to shiver. She wrung out the cloth and folded it over the faucet, then patted herself dry with a dish towel. Then, pretending to be examining her fingernails, she turned and walked over to the window. She looked up.

There he was. Her glance of a quarter of an hour ago had registered dark hair and a white shirt. Now she saw a long, older face . . . a man in his fifties maybe. A green tie. She had seen him before this morning — quick, disinterested (or so she had thought) sightings of a man in his kitchen, watching television, going from room to room. A bachelor living next door. She pressed the palms of her hands on the window, and he stepped back into shadow.

The pane clouded from her breath. She leaned her body into it, flattening her breasts against the cool glass. Right at the window she was visible to his apartment and the one below, which had closed vertical blinds. "Each window like a pill'ry appears," she thought. Vaguely appropriate lines

212

from the poems she had read last year were always occurring to her. She felt that he was still watching, but she yearned for proof.

When it became evident that he wasn't going to show himself, she went into the bedroom. The bedroom windows didn't face the apartment house, but she closed them anyway, then got into bed under the covers. Between her legs there was such a tender throbbing that she had to push a pillow into her crotch. Sex addicts must feel like this, she thought. Rapists, child molesters.

She said to herself, "You are a certifiable exhibitionist." She let out an amazed, almost exultant laugh, but instantly fell into a darker amazement as it dawned on her that she really was . . . she really *was* an exhibitionist. And what's more, she had been one for years, or at least she had been working up to being one for years.

Why, for instance, did she and Claude live here, in this vulgar low-rise? Wasn't it because of the floor-to-ceiling windows that faced the windows of the house next door?

And what about when she was twelve and became so obsessed with the idea of urinating on people's lawns that one night she crept out of the house after everyone was asleep and did it, peed on the lawn of the townhouses next door . . . right under a streetlight, in fact.

What about two years ago, when she didn't wear underpants the entire summer? She'd had a minor yeast infection and had read that it was a good idea not to wear underpants at home, if you could help it, but she had stopped wearing

213

them in public as well, beneath skirts and dresses, at parties, on buses, and she must have known that this was taking it a bit far, because she had kept it from Claude.

"Oh, my God," she said wretchedly.

She went still, alerted by how theatrical that had sounded. Her heart was beating in her throat. She touched a finger to it. So fragile, a throat. She imagined the man being excited by her hands on her throat.

What was going on? What was the matter with her? Maybe she was too aroused to be shocked at herself. She moved her hips, rubbing her crotch against the pillow. No, she didn't want to masturbate. That would ruin it.

Ruin what?

She closed her eyes, and the man appeared to her. She experienced a rush of wild longing. It was as if, all her life, she had been waiting for a long-faced, middle-aged man in a white shirt and green tie. He was probably still standing in his living room, watching her window.

She sat up, threw off the covers.

Dropped back down on the bed.

This was crazy. This really was crazy. What if he was a rapist? What if, right this minute, he was downstairs, finding out her name from the mailbox? Or what if he was just some lonely, normal man who took her display as an invitation to phone her up and ask her for a date? It's not as if she wanted to go out with him. She wasn't looking for an affair.

For an hour or so she fretted, and then she drifted off to sleep. When she woke up, shortly after noon, she was quite calm. The state she had worked herself into earlier struck her as overwrought. So, she gave some guy a thrill, so what? She was a bit of an exhibitionist . . . most women were, she bet. It was instinctive, a side effect of being the receptor in the sex act.

She decided to have lunch and go for a walk. While she was making herself a sandwich she avoided glancing at the window, but as soon as she sat at the table, she couldn't resist looking over.

He wasn't there, and yet she felt that he was watching her, standing out of sight. She ran a hand through her hair. "For Christ's sake," she reproached herself, but she was already with him. Again it was as if her eyes were in his head, although not replacing his eyes. She knew that he wanted her to slip her hand down her sweatpants. She did this. Watching his window, she removed her hand and licked her wet fingers. At that instant she would have paid money for some sign that he was watching.

After a few minutes she began to chew on her fingernails. She was suddenly depressed. She reached over and pulled the curtain across the window and ate her sandwich. Her mouth, biting into the bread, trembled like an old lady's. "Trembled like a guilty thing surprised," she quoted to herself. It wasn't guilt, though, it wasn't frustration, either, not sexual frustration. She was acquainted with this bleached sadness — it came upon her at the height of sensation . . . after orgasms, after a day of trying on clothes in stores.

She finished her sandwich and went for a long walk in her new toreador pants and her tight, black, turtleneck sweater. By the time she returned, Claude was home. He asked her if she had worked in the nude again.

"Of course," she said absently. "I have to." She was looking past him at the man's closed drapes. "Claude," she said, suddenly, "am I beautiful? I mean not just to you. Am I empirically beautiful?"

Claude looked surprised. "Well, yeah," he said. "Sure you are. Hell, I married you, didn't I? Hey!" He stepped back. "Whoa!"

She was removing her clothes. When she was naked, she said, "Don't think of me as your wife. Just as a woman. One of your patients. Am I beautiful or not?"

He made a show of eyeing her up and down. "Not bad," he said. "Of course, it depends on what you mean by 'beautiful.' " He laughed. "What's going on?"

"I'm serious. You don't think I'm kind of . . . normal? You know, plain?"

"Of course not," he said lovingly. He reached for her and drew her into his arms. "You want hard evidence?" he said.

They went into the bedroom. It was dark because the curtains were still drawn. She switched on the bedside lamp, but once he was undressed, he switched it off again.

"No," she said from the bed, "leave it on."

"What? You want it on?"

"For a change."

The next morning she got up before he did. She had hardly slept. During breakfast she kept looking over at the apartment house, but there was no sign of the man. Which didn't necessarily mean that he wasn't there. She couldn't wait for Claude to leave so that she could stop pretending she wasn't keyed up. It was gnawing at her that she had overestimated or somehow misread the man's interest. How did she know? He might be gay. He might be so devoted to a certain woman that all other women repelled him. He might be puritanical . . . a priest, a born-again Christian. He might be out of his mind.

The minute Claude was out the door, she undressed and began work on the painting. She stood in the sunlight mixing colors, then sat on the chair in her stretching pose, looking at herself in the mirror, then stood up and — without paying much attention, glancing every few seconds at his window — painted ribs and uplifted breasts.

An hour went by before she thought, he's not going to show up. She dropped into the chair, weak with disappointment, even though she knew that, very likely, he had simply been obliged to go to work, that his being home yesterday was a fluke. Forlornly she gazed at her painting. To her surprise she had accomplished something rather interesting: breasts like Picasso eyes. It is possible, she thought dully, that I am a natural talent.

She put her brush in the turpentine, and her face in her hands. She felt the sun on her hair. In a few minutes the sun would disappear behind his house, and after that, if she wanted him to get a good look at her, she would have to stand right at the window. She envisioned herself stationed there all day. You are ridiculous, she told herself. You are unhinged.

She glanced up at the window again.

He was there.

She sat up straight. Slowly she came to her feet. Stay, she prayed. He did. She walked over to the window, her fingertips brushing her thighs. She held her breath. When she was at the window, she stood perfectly still. He had on a white shirt again, but no tie. He was close enough that she could make out the darkness around his eyes, although she couldn't tell exactly where he was looking. But his eyes seemed to enter her head like a drug, and she felt herself aligned with his perspective. She saw herself — surprisingly slender, composed but apprehensive — through the glass and against the backdrop of the room's white walls.

After a minute or two she walked over to the chair, picked it up, and carried it to the window. She sat facing him, her knees apart. He was as still as a picture. So was she, because she had suddenly remembered that he might be gay or crazy. She tried to give him a hard look. She observed his age and his sad, respectable appearance . . . and the fact that he remained at the window, revealing his interest.

No, he was the man she had imagined. I am a gift to him, she thought, opening her legs wider. I am his dream come true. She began to rotate her hips. With the fingers of both hands she spread her labia.

One small part of her mind, clinging to the person she had been until yesterday morning, tried to pull her back. She felt it as a presence behind the chair, a tableau of sensational, irrelevant warnings that she was obviously not about to turn around for. She kept her eyes on the man. Moving her left hand up to her breasts, she began to rub and squeeze and to circle her fingers on the nipples. The middle finger of her right hand slipped into her vagina, as the palm massaged her clitoris.

He was motionless.

You are kissing me, she thought. She seemed to feel his lips, cool, soft, sliding, and sucking down her stomach. You are kissing me. She imagined his hands under her, lifting her like a bowl to his lips.

She was coming.

Her body jolted. Her legs shook. She had never experienced anything like it. Seeing what he saw, she witnessed an act of shocking vulnerability. It went on and on. She saw the charity of her display, her lavish recklessness and submission. It inspired her to the tenderest self-love. The man did not move, not until she had finally stopped moving, and then he reached up one hand — to signal, she thought, but it was to close the drapes.

She stayed sprawled in the chair. She was astonished. She couldn't believe herself. She couldn't believe him. How did he know to stay so still, to simply watch her? She avoided the thought that right at this moment he was probably masturbating. She absorbed herself only with what she had seen, which was a dead-still man whose eyes she had sensed roving over her body the way that eyes in certain portraits seem to follow you around a room.

The next three mornings everything was the same. He had on his white shirt, she masturbated in the chair, he watched without moving, she came spectacularly, he closed the drapes.

Afterward she went out clothes shopping or visiting people. Everyone told her how great she looked. At night she was passionate in bed, prompting Claude to ask several times, "What the hell's come over you?" but he asked it happily, he didn't look a gift horse in the mouth. She felt very loving toward Claude, not out of guilt but out of high spirits. She knew better than to confess, of course, and yet she didn't believe that she was betraying him with the man next door. A man who hadn't touched her or spoken to her, who, as far as she was concerned, only existed from the waist up and who never moved except to pull his drapes, how could that man be counted as a lover?

The fourth day, Friday, the man didn't appear. For two hours she waited in the chair. Finally she moved to the couch and watched television, keeping one eye on his window. She told herself that he must have had an urgent appointment, or that he had to go to work early. She was worried, though. At some point, late in the afternoon when she wasn't looking, he closed his drapes.

Saturday and Sunday he didn't seem to be home — the drapes were drawn and the lights off . . . not that she could have done anything anyway, not with Claude there. On Monday morning she was in her chair, naked, as soon as Claude left the house. She waited until 10:30, then put on her toreador pants and white, push-up halter top and went for a walk. A consoling line from *Romeo and Juliet* played in her head: "He that is stricken blind cannot forget the precious treasure of his eyesight lost." She was angry with the man for not being as keen as she was. If he was at his window tomorrow, she vowed she would shut her drapes on him.

But how would she replace him, what would she do? Become a table dancer? She had to laugh. Aside from the fact that she was a respectably married woman and could not dance to save her life and was probably ten years too old, the last thing she wanted was a bunch of slack-jawed, flat-eyed drunks grabbing at her breasts. She wanted one man, and she wanted him to have a sad, intelligent demeanor and the control to watch her without moving a muscle. She wanted him to wear a white shirt.

On the way home, passing his place, she stopped. The building was a mansion turned into luxury apartments. He must have money, she realized . . . an obvious conclusion, but until now she'd had no interest whatsoever in who he was.

She climbed the stairs and tried the door. Found it open. Walked in.

The mailboxes were numbered one to four. His would be four. She read the name in the little window: "Dr. Andrew Halsey."

Back at her apartment she looked him up under "Physicians" in the phone book and found that, like Claude, he was a surgeon. A general surgeon, though, a remover of tumors and diseased organs. Presumably on call. Presumably dedicated, as a general surgeon had to be.

She guessed she would forgive his absences.

The next morning and the next, Andrew (as she now thought of him) was at the window. Thursday he wasn't. She tried not to be disappointed. She imagined him saving

221

people's lives, drawing his scalpel along skin in beautifully precise cuts. For something to do she worked on her painting. She painted fishlike eyes, a hooked nose, a mouth full of teeth. She worked fast.

Andrew was there Friday morning. When Ali saw him she rose to her feet and pressed her body against the window, as she had done the first morning. Then she walked to the chair, turned it around and leaned over it, her back to him. She masturbated stroking herself from behind.

That afternoon she bought him a pair of binoculars, an expensive, powerful pair, which she wrapped in brown paper, addressed, and left on the floor in front of his mailbox. All weekend she was preoccupied with wondering whether he would understand that she had given them to him and whether he would use them. She had considered including a message: "For our mornings" or something like that, but such direct communication seemed like a violation of a pact between them. The binoculars alone were a risk.

Monday, before she even had her housecoat off, he walked from the rear of the room to the window, the binoculars at his eyes. Because most of his face was covered by the binoculars and his hands, she had the impression that he was masked. Her legs shook. When she opened her legs and spread her labia, his eyes crawled up her. She masturbated but didn't come and didn't try to, although she put on a show of coming. She was so devoted to his appreciation that her pleasure seemed like a siphoning of his, an early, childish indulgence that she would never return to.

It was later, with Claude, that she came. After supper

she pulled him onto the bed. She pretended that he was Andrew, or rather she imagined a dark, long-faced, silent man who made love with his eyes open but who smelled and felt like Claude and whom she loved and trusted as she did Claude. With this hybrid partner she was able to relax enough to encourage the kind of kissing and movement she needed but had never had the confidence to insist upon. The next morning, masturbating for Andrew, she reached the height of ecstasy, as if her orgasms with him had been the fantasy, and her pretenses of orgasm were the real thing. Not coming released her completely into his dream of her. The whole show was for him — cunt, ass, mouth, throat offered to his magnified vision.

For several weeks Andrew turned up regularly, five mornings a week, and she lived in a state of elation. In the afternoons she worked on her painting, without much concentration though, since finishing it didn't seem to matter anymore in spite of how well it was turning out. Claude insisted that it was still very much a self-portrait, a statement Ali was insulted by, given the woman's obvious primitivism and her flat, distant eyes.

There was no reason for her to continue working in the nude, but she did, out of habit and comfort, and on the outside chance that Andrew might be peeking through his drapes. While she painted she wondered about her exhibitionism, what it was about her that craved to have a strange man look at her. Of course, everyone and everything liked to be looked at to a certain degree, she thought. Flowers, cats, anything that preened or shone, children crying, "Look at me!" Some mornings her episodes with Andrew seemed to have nothing at all to do with lust; they were completely display, wholehearted surrender to what felt like the most inaugural and genuine of all desires, which was not sex but which happened to be expressed through a sexual act.

One night she dreamed that Andrew was operating on her. Above the surgical mask his eyes were expressionless. He had very long arms. She was also able to see, as if through his eyes, the vertical incision that went from between her breasts to her navel, and the skin on either side of the incision folded back like a scroll. Her heart was brilliant red and perfectly heart-shaped. All of her other organs were glistening yellows and oranges. Somebody should take a picture of this, she thought. Andrew's gloved hands barely appeared to move as they wielded long, silver instruments. There was no blood on his hands. Very carefully, so that she hardly felt it, he prodded her organs and plucked at her veins and tendons, occasionally drawing a tendon out and dropping it into a petri dish. It was as if he were weeding a garden. Her heart throbbed. A tendon encircled her heart, and when he pulled on it she could feel that its other end encircled her vagina, and the uncoiling there was the most exquisite sensation she had ever experienced. She worried that she would come and that her trembling and spasms would cause him to accidentally stab her. She woke up coming.

All day the dream obsessed her. It *could* happen, she reasoned. She could have a gall bladder or an appendicitis attack and be rushed to the hospital and, just as she was going under, see that the surgeon was Andrew. It could happen.

When she woke up the next morning, the dream was her first thought. She looked down at the gentle swell of her stomach and felt sentimental and excited. She found it impossible to shake the dream, even while she was masturbating for Andrew, so that instead of entering *his* dream of her, instead of seeing a naked woman sitting in a pool of morning sun, she saw her sliced-open chest in the shaft of his surgeon's light. Her heart was what she focused on, its fragile pulsing, but she also saw the slower rise and fall of her lungs, and the quivering of her other organs. Between her organs were tantalizing crevices and entwined swirls of blue and red — her veins and arteries. Her tendons were seashell pink, threaded tight as guitar strings.

Of course she realized that she had the physiology all wrong and that in a real operation there would be blood and pain and she would be anesthetized. It was an impossible, mad fantasy; she didn't expect it to last. But every day it became more enticing as she authenticated it with hard data, such as the name of the hospital he operated out of (she called his number in the phone book and asked his nurse) and the name of the surgical instruments he would use (she consulted one of Claude's medical texts), and as she smoothed out the rough edges by imagining, for instance, minuscule suction tubes planted here and there in the incision to remove every last drop of blood.

In the mornings, during her real encounters with Andrew,

she became increasingly frustrated until it was all she could do not to quit in the middle, close the drapes, or walk out of the room. And yet if he failed to show up, she was desperate. She started to drink gin and tonics before lunch and to sunbathe at the edge of the driveway between her building and his, knowing he wasn't home from ten o'clock on, but laying there for hours, just in case.

One afternoon, lightheaded from gin and sun, restless with worry because he hadn't turned up the last three mornings, she changed out of her bikini and into a strapless, cotton dress and went for a walk. She walked past the park she had been heading for, past the stores she had thought she might browse in. The sun bore down. Strutting by men who eyed her bare shoulders, she felt voluptuous, sweetly rounded. But at the pit of her stomach was a filament of anxiety, evidence that despite telling herself otherwise, she knew where she was going.

She entered the hospital by the Emergency doors and wandered the corridors for what seemed like half an hour before discovering Andrew's office. By this time she was holding her stomach and half believing that the feeling of anxiety might actually be a symptom of something very serious.

"Dr. Halsey isn't seeing patients," his nurse said. She slit open a manila envelope with a lion's head letter opener. "They'll take care of you at Emergency."

"I have to see Dr. Halsey," Ali said, her voice cracking. "I'm a friend."

The nurse sighed. "Just a minute." She stood and went

down a hall, opening a door at the end after a quick knock.

Ali pressed her fists into her stomach. For some reason she no longer felt a thing. She pressed harder. What a miracle if she burst her appendix! She should stab herself with the letter opener. She should at least break her fingers, slam them in a drawer like a draft dodger.

"Would you like to come in?" a high, nasal voice said. Ali spun around. It was Andrew, standing at the door.

"The doctor will see you," the nurse said impatiently, sitting back behind her desk.

Ali's heart began to pound. She felt as if a pair of hands were cupping and uncupping her ears. His shirt was blue. She went down the hall, squeezing past him without looking up, and sat in the green plastic chair beside his desk. He shut the door and walked over to the window. It was a big room; there was a long expanse of old green and yellow floor tiles between them. Leaning his hip against a filing cabinet, he just stood there, hands in his trouser pockets, regarding her with such a polite, impersonal expression that she asked him if he recognized her.

"Of course I do," he said quietly.

"Well—" Suddenly she was mortified. She felt like a woman about to sob that she couldn't afford the abortion. She touched her fingers to her hot face.

"I don't know your name," he said.

"Oh. Ali. Ali Perrin."

"What do you want, Ali?"

Her eyes fluttered down to his shoes—black, shabby loafers. She hated his adenoidal voice. What did she want?

What she wanted was to bolt from the room like the mad woman she suspected she was. She glanced up at him again. Because he was standing with his back to the window, he was outlined in light. It made him seem unreal, like a film image superimposed against a screen. She tried to look away, but his eyes held her. Out in the waiting room the telephone was ringing. What do *you* want, she thought, capitulating to the pull of her perspective over to his, seeing now, from across the room, a charming woman with tanned, bare shoulders and blushing cheeks.

The light blinked on his phone. Both of them glanced over at it, but he stayed standing where he was. After a moment she murmured, "I have no idea what I'm doing here."

He was silent. She kept her eyes on the phone, waiting for him to speak. When he didn't, she said, "I had a dream . . ." She let out a disbelieving laugh. "God." She shook her head.

"You are very lovely," he said in a speculative tone. She glanced up at him, and he turned away. Pressing his hands together, he took a few steps along the window. "I have very much enjoyed our . . . our encounters," he said.

"Oh, don't worry," she said. "I'm not here to —"

"However," he cut in, "I should tell you that I am moving into another building."

She looked straight at him.

"This weekend, as a matter of fact." He frowned at his wall of framed diplomas.

"This weekend?" she said.

"Yes."

"So," she murmured. "It's over then."

"Regrettably."

She stared at his profile. In profile he was a stranger — beak-nosed, round-shouldered. She hated his shoes, his floor, his formal way of speaking, his voice, his profile, and yet her eyes filled and she longed for him to look at her again.

Abruptly he turned his back to her and said that his apartment was in the east end, near the beach. He gestured out the window. Did she know where the yacht club was?

"No," she whispered.

"Not that I am a member," he said with a mild laugh.

"Listen," she said, wiping her eyes. "I'm sorry." She came to her feet. "I guess I just wanted to see you."

He strode like an obliging host over to the door.

"Well, good-bye," she said, looking up into his face.

He had garlic breath and five o'clock shadow. His eyes grazed hers. "I wouldn't feel too badly about anything," he said affably.

When she got back to the apartment the first thing she did was take her clothes off and go over to the full-length mirror, which was still standing next to the easel. Her eyes filled again because without Andrew's appreciation or the hope of it (and despite how repellent she had found him) what she saw was a pathetic little woman with pasty skin and short legs.

She looked at the painting. If *that* was her, as Claude claimed, then she also had flat eyes and crude, wild proportions.

What on earth did Claude see in her?

What had Andrew seen? "You are very lovely," Andrew had said, but maybe he'd been reminding himself. Maybe he'd meant, "lovely when I'm in the next building."

After supper that evening she asked Claude to lie with her on the couch, and the two of them watched TV. She held his hand against her breast. "Let this be enough," she prayed.

But she didn't believe it ever would be. The world was too full of surprises, it frightened her. As Claude was always saying, things looked different from different angles, and in different lights. What this meant to her was that everything hinged on where you happened to be standing at a given moment, or even on who you imagined you were. It meant that in certain lights, desire sprang up out of nowhere.

Author's Note: "Ninety-Three Million Miles Away" was conceived as a response to Alberto Moravia's novel, *The Voyeur.* I wanted to turn the perspective around and write from the viewpoint of the object rather than the subject, although in so doing I made the (perhaps obvious) discovery that the object of desire is simultaneously the subject.

I also wanted to write a story about teetering on the edge, so I let my exhibitionist take her fantasy right to its logical extreme.

CONTRIBUTOR NOTes

BLAKE C. AARENS has had short stories published in the literary magazine *Open Wide*, in *Aché*, a journal for lesbians of African descent, and *Herotica 2* and *3*. She lives in Oakland, California, with her cat Sonja, and is hard at work on her first novel, tentatively titled *Faith Hope and Tragedy*.

NICHOLSON BAKER has published three novels and a work of criticism. His work has appeared in *The New Yorker*, *The Atlantic* and *Esquire*. He lives in northern California with his wife and child.

GREG BOYD is a writer, visual artist, and publisher of Asylum Arts Books. His most recent book is a collection of short fiction and photo collage entitled *Carnival Aptitude*.

PAT CALIFIA's erotic fiction has featured people of all genders and sexual orientations. She is the author of *Sapphistry* (Naiad), *Macho Sluts, Doc and Fluff, The Lesbian S/M Safety Manual,* and a collection of her *Advocate Advisor* columns (all Alyson Publications). Her forthcoming works include a new short story collection, *Melting Point,* and an S/M sex manual, *Sensual Magic* (Masquerade). She is currently editing a collection of short stories: *Doing It for Daddy,* with Robin Sweeney, and a sequel to the lesbian S/M anthology, *Coming to Power,* entitled *The Second Coming.*

SAMUEL R. DELANY is the author of numerous books of fiction, criticism, and non-fiction. He teaches at the University of Massachusetts, Amherst.

MICHAEL DORSEY is a writer and actor living in New York City. "Milk" is his first published short story.

BOB FLANAGAN is the author of several books of poetry and prose including *The Wedding of Everything, Slave Sonnets* and *Fuck Journal.* Selections from his current work in progress, *The Book of Medicine,* have appeared in numerous journals and anthologies, including *High Risk* (Dutton/Plume). His most recent work, with collaborator Sheree Rose, was "Visiting Hours," an installation at the Santa Monica Museum of Art which dealt with Bob's lifelong battle with cystic fibrosis and its influence on his sexuality.

BARBARA GOWDY is the author of two novels, *Through the Grass Valley* and *Falling Angels,* as well as a story collection, *We So Seldom Look on Love,* which includes the new version of "Ninety-three Million Miles Away." A full-time writer and editor, her books have been published in nine countries and seven languages. She lives in Toronto.

ANN MARIE MARDITH lives in Minnesota where you must find love before November or do without until May since no one comes out of their houses before then. She is grateful to her sisters who encouraged her to write.

ANITA "MELISSA" MASHMAN and Paradigm Press feel it's time to set a fat-positive example and publish tales of fat women doing all those things that society says we can't or aren't allowed to: dancing, running, thinking (especially about things other than food), looking good, attracting love, and indulging in mad, passionate (sometimes kinky) lust.

MAGENTA MICHAELS is a poet and handbook binder. She lives on the coast south of San Francisco with her husband. "Rubenesque" is her first published short story.

LISA PALAC is the editor of *Future Sex* magazine and producer of *Cyborgasm,* a collection of erotic sessions recorded in Virtual 3-D Audio.

CAROL A. QUEEN did grow up queer in a small town; she only wishes *The Golden Boy* were a true story. It was never quite that exciting. However, she is indebted to the gay schoolteacher who loaned her *Song of the Loon.* Today she is a writer and sex educator in San Francisco, giving special focus to marginalized sexualities.

ANNE RICE was born in New Orleans, where she now lives with her husband, the poet Stan Rice, and their son, Christopher.

LEIGH RUTLEDGE is the author of *The Gay Book of Lists*, *Unnatural Quotations*, *The Gay Fireside Companion* and *The Gay Decades*. He is also the author of *The Lefthanders' Guide to Life*, and several humor books.

ROBERT SILVERBERG, a prolific San Francisco writer and six-time Nebula winner, has been a frequent contributor to Penthouse Special Publications.

RONALD SUKENICK is publisher of *American Book Review* and the author of numerous works of fiction and criticism. He has recently completed a long novel about Jewish experience in the 20th century, from which the selection included here is an excerpt.

TRISH THOMAS is a fairly studly white trash bar dyke who writes the way she talks. Her work has been banned in Canada and has appeared in several magazines, including *Taste of Latex*, *Quim*, *Bad Attitude*, *SF Weekly*, and in two anthologies: *Dagger* (Cleis), and *The Girl Wants To* (Coach House Press).

PAT A. WILLIAMS, born and raised in rural west Tennessee, is presently at work on a Black Panther novel, an exploration of a revolutionary feminist woman.

CARTER WILSON is the author of four novels, including *Treasures on Earth* and *Crazy February*. He worked on the narration for two Oscar-winning films, *The Times of Harvey Milk* and *Common Threads*.

READERS' DIRECTORY

·

Many of the stories in *Best American Erotica 1993* were first published in the following magazines, journals and 'zines which regularly include or emphasize erotic literature.

Aché
A Journal For Lesbians of African Descent. Published at P.O. Box 6071, Albany, CA 94706.

Fiction International 22
Harold Jaffe and Larry McCafferty, Editors. Published biannually at San Diego State University Press, San Diego State University, San Diego, CA 92182. Subscriptions are $14 per year.

Frighten the Horses
A document of the sexual revolution. Mark Pritchard and

Cris Gutierrez, Co-editors. Published quarterly at 41 Sutter St. #1108, San Francisco, CA 94104. Subscriptions are $18 for four issues.

Lavender Reader
News & Reviews for Santa Cruz County's Gay and Lesbian Community. Jo Kenny and Scott Brookie, Editors. Published quarterly at P.O. Box 7293, Santa Cruz, CA 95061. Subscriptions are $12 per year.

Libido
The Journal of Sex and Sensibility. Marianna Beck and Jack Hafferkamp, Editors/Publishers. Published quarterly at P.O. Box 146721, Chicago, IL 60614. Subscriptions are $26 per year; $36 in Canada and Mexico; $46 in Europe; $56 elsewhere.

Penthouse Letters
The Magazine of Sexual Marvels. Don Myrus, Editor. Published monthly at 1965 Broadway, New York, NY 10023-5965. Subscriptions are $28 per year; $38 in Canada and elsewhere.

Screw
Al Goldstein, Editor/Publisher. Published weekly at 432 Old Chelsea St., New York, NY 10113. Subscriptions are $75 for 52 issues, $45 for 26 issues.

Taste of Latex
Lily Braindrop, Editor/Publisher. Published quarterly at P.O. Box 460122, San Francisco, CA 94146. Subscriptions are $20 per year.

CREDITS

·

SUSIE BRIGHT edited *Herotica* (Down There Press) and the best-selling *Herotica 2* (Plume), a collection of women's erotica, and she is the author of *Sexual Reality* and *Susi Sexpert's Lesbian Sex World* (both from Cleis Press). She has lectured internationally and toured the country with her multimedia presentation, "How to Read a Dirty Movie." Her work has appeared in numerous magazines, journals and newspapers, including *Esquire, Rolling Stone, Elle, The Advocate, Penthouse, The New York Times Book Review* and *The San Francisco Review of Books. Minneapolis Weekly* named Susie Bright number 23 among their "62 Reasons to Love America."